He awoke with a w

Even with his eyes closed, Talbot felt the warm, feminine body curled against him, and his nose was filled with the heady scent of sweet strawberries. As he drew in a breath, he suddenly remembered. The crash…Elizabeth…the forest. His eyes snapped open and he saw that at some point in the night, their bodies had not only sought the soft, leaf-covered ground but each other's.

Her face was turned toward his, and he took the opportunity to study her with the glow of morning dawn seeping through the trees. He could easily understand why his brother had been so enthralled with her. She was lovely, with sinfully thick lashes and an inviting mouth that urged a man to plunder its depths. His finger itched to caress her cheek, touch her full bottom lip.…

He wanted her. For years, he'd wanted her—and in that desire had been his shame.

Elizabeth McCarthy was—and would always be— his brother's woman.

Dear Reader,

The year is off to a wonderful start in Silhouette Romance, and we've got some of our best stories yet for you right here.

Our tremendously successful ROYALLY WED series continues with *The Blacksheep Prince's Bride* by Martha Shields. Our intrepid heroine—a lady-in-waiting for Princess Isabel—will do anything to help rescue the king. Even marry the single dad turned prince! And Judy Christenberry returns to Romance with *Newborn Daddy*. Poor Ryan didn't know what he was missing, until he looked through the nursery window....

Also this month, Teresa Southwick concludes her much-loved series about the Marchetti family in *The Last Marchetti Bachelor*. And popular author Elizabeth August gives us *Slade's Secret Son*. Lisa hadn't planned to tell Slade about their child. But with her life in danger, there's only one man to turn to....

Carla Cassidy's tale of love and adventure is *Lost in His Arms*, while new-to-the-Romance-line Vivienne Wallington proves she's anything but a beginning writer in this powerful story of a man *Claiming His Bride*.

Be sure to come back next month for Valerie Parv's ROYALLY WED title as well as new stories by Sandra Steffen and Myrna Mackenzie. And Patricia Thayer will begin a brand-new series, THE TEXAS BROTHERHOOD.

Happy reading!

Mary-Theresa Hussey

Mary-Theresa Hussey
Senior Editor

Please address questions and book requests to:
Silhouette Reader Service
U.S.: 3010 Walden Ave., P.O. Box 1325, Buffalo, NY 14269
Canadian: P.O. Box 609, Fort Erie, Ont. L2A 5X3

Lost in His Arms

CARLA CASSIDY

SILHOUETTE *Romance*®

Published by Silhouette Books

America's Publisher of Contemporary Romance

SILHOUETTE BOOKS

ISBN 0-373-19514-1

LOST IN HIS ARMS

Copyright © 2001 by Carla Bracale

This edition published by arrangement with Harlequin Books S.A.

® and TM are trademarks of Harlequin Books S.A., used under license.
Trademarks indicated with ® are registered in the United States Patent
and Trademark Office, the Canadian Trade Marks Office and in other
countries.

Visit Silhouette at www.eHarlequin.com

Printed in U.S.A.

Books by Carla Cassidy

CARLA CASSIDY

is an award-winning author who has written over thirty-five books for Silhouette. In 1995, she won Best Silhouette Romance from *Romantic Times Magazine* for *Anything for Danny*. In 1998, she also won a Career Achievement Award for Best Innovative Series from *Romantic Times Magazine*.

Carla believes the only thing better than curling up with a good book to read is sitting down at the computer with a good story to write. She's looking forward to writing many more books and bringing hours of pleasure to readers.

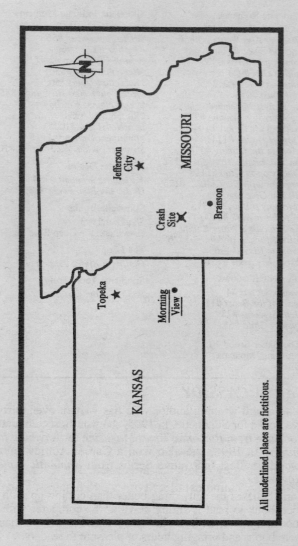

MISSOURI

Jefferson City ★

Crash Site ✕

Branson ●

Topeka ★

Morning View ●

KANSAS

All underlined places are fictitious.

Chapter One

Talbot McCarthy was not a happy camper.

Seated in his single-engine Cessna, ready for take-off, he glanced quickly at the woman in the seat next to him. Her tawny hair shone with rich highlights as the last of the day's sun danced in through the windows.

It had been almost a year since he'd seen her, but time hadn't dulled the intense blue of her eyes or softened the determined thrust of her chin.

Elizabeth McCarthy.

His brother's ex-wife.

Before they'd left her apartment, she'd changed from her feminine, tailored dress into a pair of jeans, a T-shirt and a windbreaker to ward off the coolness of the early-autumn evening.

The jeans clung to her long slender legs, and the pale tangerine-colored T-shirt reflected the color of peaches onto her cheeks. He tried not to notice the thrust of her breasts against the cotton fabric.

She looked totally relaxed and self-possessed as they awaited takeoff. Then he spied her hands. They were clasped together in her lap, connected so tightly that her knuckles and fingers had turned white.

"You don't like to fly?" he asked, guessing at the cause of her obvious distress.

"Not particularly," she replied, her voice breathy with tension. "If I must fly, I prefer big commercial planes, not planes no bigger than my bathroom."

"Don't worry, I'm an excellent pilot," he said.

"Yeah, and the *Titanic* was unsinkable."

At that moment the tower gave him the okay for takeoff. He turned onto the runway and taxied to a high enough speed to begin his ascent.

He didn't speak to her again until they had reached their cruising altitude. "You can relax now. It should be smooth sailing from here to Branson."

Her hands unclasped and she drew a deep breath, audible above the drone of the engine. "Do you fly often?"

"Fairly regularly," he replied. "As CEO of McCarthy Industries, there's always a meeting to attend or some troubleshooting to be done at one of our branch offices. I got tired of depending on airline schedules, and I like the independence of flying my own plane.''

He could tell she was only half listening to him and knew her thoughts would be for her nine-year-old son, Andrew, and her ex-husband. ''I wish I could tell you what Richard was thinking when he pulled this latest stunt.''

A small smile curved one corner of her generous mouth, and Talbot tightened his grip on the controls, trying to ignore how the gesture softened her features and made her more beautiful than he'd have thought possible.

''You and I have never had much luck at second-guessing Richard and his stunts.''

''That's an understatement,'' he agreed. He focused his attention away from her and frowned. He had no idea what his younger brother was up to this time. All he knew was that Richard had picked up his son from school that afternoon, without checking with Elizabeth, on a weekend that wasn't his usual visitation time.

When she'd gotten home from work, Elizabeth had found a note on her kitchen table that indicated Richard wanted her to go to Twin Oaks, Missouri, a small town just outside Branson, where Richard and Talbot had spent their childhood.

Elizabeth had called Talbot to see if he knew what was going on. Talbot insisted he fly from his home in Morning View, Kansas, to Kansas City. He'd picked up Elizabeth at her apartment and they were now on their way to Twin Oaks.

Talbot suspected that, as usual, they were victims of his impetuous brother and one of his spontaneous thoughtless stunts.

Next to him, Elizabeth shifted position, and he caught a whiff of her perfume. Subtle yet sexy. She'd worn that scent for as long as he could remember. In fact, she'd been wearing it the very first night he'd met her, when she and Richard had come to Talbot to tell him she was pregnant and they were getting married.

Richard had looked scared to death, but Elizabeth's blue eyes had radiated strength and purpose, and to Talbot's shame, he had felt a flicker of envy that his younger brother had found such a beautiful, strong young woman to claim as his own.

He'd been appalled by that momentary stab of jealousy, and had consciously attempted to hold himself distant from her in the years of her marriage to Richard. In fact, he'd often been cold and brusque with her.

He'd hoped that attraction had died, but catching the scent of her familiar perfume, he was acutely aware of her presence next to him and of a tiny flame of heat that had ignited somewhere in the pit of his stomach.

Richard's woman, he reminded himself. And even though she and Richard had been divorced for a year, she would never be anything other than Rich-ard's woman.

"I should be beside myself with anger at Richard for this," she said, interrupting his thoughts. "But I've always found it hard to sustain anger toward Richard for any length of time."

This time Talbot felt a smile curving his lips. "Yeah, I know what you mean." Despite Richard's immaturity and thoughtlessness, there was some-thing endearing about him that made it difficult to get really angry with him. He was like a little boy who probably needed a spanking, but usually got away with nothing more than a sigh of exasperation from the adults around him.

Talbot's smile faded and he frowned thoughtfully. "But he hasn't been himself this past week."

"What do you mean?"

Talbot felt her gaze on him, but didn't turn to look at her. He'd learned through the years that looking at her was dangerous. It often resulted in inappro-priate thoughts.

"I don't know… He's been unusually quiet, and when he does talk, lately all he talks about is our childhood…the past."

"Maybe he's doing some growing up, at twenty-seven. He's still working for you at McCarthy In-dustries, right?"

Talbot nodded. "He's a good personnel manager. He's good with people."

Talbot wondered if perhaps Richard was regretting his divorce from Elizabeth, and if this trip to Twin Oaks might not be an attempt to forge a reconciliation.

Richard probably hadn't expected Elizabeth to call his older brother. But she had, to see if he knew what Richard was up to.

It had been Talbot's idea to fly her to Branson where they could rent a car and drive to the tiny town of Twin Oaks. She'd readily agreed, preferring an hour-long plane trip to a four-and-a-half-hour trip in a car.

He wondered if Richard did want reconciliation, would Elizabeth be willing to try the marriage again? Certainly Andrew would be pleased if such a thing happened. Although he seemed well-adjusted to the divorce, wasn't it every child's dream to see his parents together?

And certainly all Talbot had ever wanted was for his brother to be happy. He'd promised his father a long time ago that he'd do everything in his power to take care of Richard.

He started as a shrill alarm screamed through the cockpit.

"What's that?" Elizabeth gasped.

Talbot stared in horror at the gas gauge. Almost empty. But that was impossible; he'd refueled before he left Morning View "I don't know. It looks like we're losing fuel."

"But we're still miles from Branson," Elizabeth protested, an edge of hysteria in her voice.

"Look outside your window and see if there's a clearing where I can put down."

"You're kidding, right?"

At that moment the engine of the plane coughed once, then stopped running.

The only sound was the rush of the wind buffeting the plane from side to side. "No, I'm not kidding," he said softly.

"What's happening?"

"The engine has stopped." Talbot worked to maintain control of the small aircraft. He picked up the microphone, but with only seconds to radio for help, he dropped it and kept his hands on the controls as the plane began to descend far too quickly.

"What do you mean, the engine has stopped?" Her voice rose slightly.

"I mean I'm no longer in control of this plane."

"That's ridiculous!" she cried. "You're always in control of everything."

At some other point in time, her comment would have warranted further discussion, but at the moment, he needed all his energy, all his focus, to keep the plane in the air. And it was a battle he was losing.

"We're going down," he said.

"I'll never forgive you for this, Talbot McCarthy!" she exclaimed just before they hit the trees.

* * *

Elizabeth had always believed there's a moment before death when your life flashes before your eyes, and all the pleasures, all the regrets mingle together for one shining moment of profound truth.

She was wrong. What flashed through her head as the plane fell from the sky were two things—a deep mourning for her son and the embarrassment of knowing she'd put on her most ragged panties that morning.

The noise when they hit the trees was deafening. Metal screeched, glass shattered, and it took a moment for Elizabeth to realize she was adding to the cacophony by screaming at the top of her lungs.

She clung to her seat as the fuselage was smashed from side to side. Her stomach heaved, as if she was riding a roller coaster and had just gone down the biggest drop. Vaguely she was aware of Talbot adding a string of colorful oaths to the thunderous noise.

Without warning, the fuselage veered sharply, then flipped on its side. Something hit Elizabeth on the side of her head, and blackness descended. Her last conscious thought was that death was surprisingly anticlimactic.

"Elizabeth?"

A male voice penetrated the black fog and disrupted her peaceful sense of nothingness. The voice came again, irritating her with its sense of urgency.

"Elizabeth!" This time she recognized the voice. Talbot. How on earth had Talbot McCarthy managed to gain entry to heaven?

Her next thought was even more disturbing. What if she hadn't made it to heaven? What if her afterlife consisted of sharing space in hell with Talbot?

A protest formed on her lips and her eyes snapped open. A new vision of hell greeted her. The darkness was pierced by a strange flickering illumination. Tangled metal...acrid smoke...a tree branch jutting through what had once been the front window.

The plane. A sharp stab of pain pierced the right side of her head as she oriented herself to where she was and what had just happened.

They'd crashed. She jerked her head to the side to look at Talbot. In the flashing light, she saw his gaze on her.

"Thank God," he said. "For a minute there, I thought you were dead. Are you all right?"

She winced and reached up to touch the side of her head, where a goose egg had risen and was incredibly tender to the pressure of her fingertips. "I think so, although for a minute, I thought I was dead, too. What about you?"

"I'm okay. But something is burning. We need to get out of here as quickly as possible." He unbuckled himself. "We'll have to go out your door. Mine won't open."

Elizabeth unfastened her seat belt and stood, unsteady on her feet as her head reeled with a sick pain. She managed to push her door open, then turned back to Talbot, who still sat in his seat.

"Are you coming?" she asked, worried now that she saw flames flaring in what was left of the plane behind them.

"My left leg seems to be trapped," he said between clenched teeth as he used his hands to tug on his leg.

Elizabeth watched him working to free himself. As the flames grew hotter, illuminating the cabin, she saw dots of perspiration above his upper lip. He cursed and yanked, half falling from his seat as the leg finally came free.

"Go!" he shouted, and pushed her toward the door.

She hesitated and stared out the opening at what was left of the plane. The wings had been torn away, leaving only the small fuselage, which was now wedged between two towering trees and suspended about eight feet from the ground.

"We're caught in the trees," she said.

"How far to the ground?" he asked, urgency apparent in his voice.

"I don't know for sure. About eight or nine feet—" Before the words had completely left her mouth, he shoved her from behind. She screamed and flailed her arms for an instant, as if by some miracle she might take flight.

She hit the ground and her knees buckled, throwing her facedown into the ground. Before she could lift her head, she heard Talbot hit the earth nearby. His landing was punctuated by a loud groan.

A moment later, he was towering over her. He grabbed her by the arm and yanked her to her feet. "We've got to get away from the plane," he said. "I don't know if it will explode or not, but we can't take the chance."

He took a step, then crumpled against her.

"You're hurt."

"I'm all right—it's just my leg. It got wrenched or something." He tried to take another step, then cursed soundly as he nearly fell. "We've got to get some distance. You're going to have to help me."

She positioned herself beneath his arm, allowing him to lean heavily on her shoulder. Step by step, they inched away from the plane, deeper into the dense forest that surrounded them.

Trees were everywhere, as were mangled parts of the plane, and as they walked away from the smoldering crash site, Elizabeth marveled at the fact that they had escaped with their lives. A few inches to the left or the right, they would have hit a tree trunk head-on, and neither of them would have survived.

"Okay, we should be far enough away now," he said when they'd moved about a hundred feet from the wreck. He eased himself to the ground, and Elizabeth sat down next to him.

Both of them stared at the burning aircraft. Flames licked hesitantly as if unwilling to fully commit to consuming the plane.

"How long before it explodes?" she asked.

"I don't know. I don't even know for sure that it will. There wasn't any fuel left, so it might not. Pray it does."

She looked at him in surprise. "Why?"

He turned to eye her, his taut features visible in the orange glow of the flames. "An explosion might be the only thing that gets somebody's attention and brings help faster. Otherwise, who knows how long it'll take for somebody to find us."

They sat watching the flames flickering here and there without actually bursting into a full inferno. With each minute that passed, the adrenaline and the shock that had momentarily gripped Elizabeth began to ebb.

Andrew. Her son's name was her first rational thought. She shivered as she realized just how close he'd come to being motherless.

She was aware of body pain where she hadn't known she had body, and her head ached with a nauseating intensity.

The night was silent, other than the crackle of the dwindling flames. And as the flames grew dimmer, the blackness of the night grew more profound. The sky wasn't visible through the tops of the trees, so no moonlight broke the descending darkness.

For the first time since the crash, she felt a flutter of fear in her stomach. "Where are we?" she asked.

"My best guess is somewhere between Kansas City and Branson."

"Well, that certainly narrows it down," she said. With the fear came a healthy dose of anger. "I thought you said you were an excellent pilot."

"I am. You aren't dead, are you?" He didn't look at her, but instead, kept his gaze focused on the last of the fire. "I'm sorry I can't be more specific about where we are."

"I guess we aren't going to make it to Twin Oaks." She desperately attempted to embrace her anger, finding it more palatable than the fear she was desperately fighting. "I can't believe this. I can't believe you crashed the plane."

"I didn't do it on purpose," he said dryly.

Her cheeks flushed and she drew a deep breath. "Of course you didn't. I'm sorry," she said grudgingly. "I'm upset."

"It must be contagious, because I'm a little upset myself." He drew a deep breath and plucked at the torn sleeve of his suit jacket. "This was my favorite suit, and now it's ruined."

She stared at him in disbelief, then saw a small curve at the corner of his mouth. "Talbot McCarthy made a joke?"

"Don't sound so surprised. I do have a sense of humor."

"You could have fooled me," she replied. "In all the years I was married to Richard, I don't think I saw you smile once." In fact, she'd always found him rigid, cold and slightly disapproving—and exceptionally attractive. That dichotomy had made her extremely uncomfortable. "So what do we do now?"

"If I had my cell phone, I'd call for help. Unfortunately it must have slipped from my pocket during the crash or when I scrambled out of the plane. So now the smartest thing to do is stay here close to the plane and hope help is on the way."

But what if help wasn't on the way, she wanted to ask. But she was afraid of what the answer might be. She scooted back so she could lean against a tree trunk, unsurprised when he followed her example and joined her.

She cast him a surreptitious glance as he leaned back and closed his eyes. Under different circumstances, she would have taken pleasure in his disheveled state.

In all the years she'd known him, she'd never seen him in such a state of disarray. His rich dark hair was tousled beyond style, and a smudge of smoke or oil decorated a cheekbone. His suit jacket was ripped and dirty, and the shirt that had been so pristine when they'd taken off was now wrinkled and blackened.

She frowned, remembering how he'd looked

when he'd first appeared on her doorstep earlier that evening. He hadn't just stood in her doorway, he'd filled it with his presence. At six foot two, Talbot had the body of a natural athlete. Broad-shouldered, slender-hipped, he carried himself with a masculine grace that drew women's attention.

However, he wasn't handsome in the traditional sense. He had bold features, dark eyes that revealed nothing of the inner man, a thin mouth that rarely smiled and a hawklike nose that gave his face a cool arrogance.

She gasped as her gaze now drifted over his legs. His slacks were torn, exposing his knee. The skin had been slashed open and the deep wound still oozed blood.

"Talbot, your knee is really hurt," she said. "It's bleeding."

He opened his eyes and looked down at his knee. "It'll be all right. It's not bleeding that badly." One eyebrow lifted as he turned his gaze to her. "Of course, if you feel the need to rip off your T-shirt and wrap my wounds, go for it."

"As if I'd sacrifice a perfectly good T-shirt for you," she scoffed. "I'll make you a deal," she continued. "If you can tear off a bunch of tree limbs and construct us a nice little lean-to to sit in while we wait for help, then I'll rip up my shirt for your leg."

He laughed, and the unfamiliar sound of his

laughter sent a familiar heat spiraling through her—
a heat that was distinctly uncomfortable.

From the moment she'd met Talbot, she'd felt a
crazy pull toward him that had been frightening.
And for the nine years of her marriage to his brother,
she had fought it. She had consciously never spent
any time at all alone with Talbot. And now they
were stuck alone together in the middle of nowhere.
She tried to ignore her disquiet.

"I think we've both seen too many movies," he
said. "Besides, I wouldn't waste a good lean-to on
you."

Although he was merely returning Elizabeth's
comment in kind, she was grateful for the slight
coolness in his voice, a coolness that reminded her
she had never been sure she even liked Talbot Mc-
Carthy.

A light flashed someplace in the distance. Elizabeth shot to her feet. "Did you see that?" she asked.
Excitement and relief ripped through her. "Maybe
it was the light from a search helicopter."

As soon as the words left her mouth, a loud rumble resounded overhead. Not the rumble of a search
plane, but rather the result of cold air meeting warm.

"I don't think it's a search helicopter," he said.
"I believe we're in for a storm."

As the first fat raindrops fell from the sky and
splattered on her upturned face, Elizabeth glared at

her companion. ''I think I hate you, Talbot McCarthy,'' she stated emphatically.

''Trust me, Elizabeth, before this is all over with, I believe the feeling just might become mutual.''

Chapter Two

Talbot had never felt so out of his element. The rain fell steadily for about an hour, effectively dousing any lingering embers that might have still been burning on the plane and getting them wet enough to be miserable.

Fortunately the storm moved on, leaving behind a profound darkness and a silence broken only by the sounds of their breathing.

"No search party will be coming tonight, will they." Elizabeth's soft voice broke the silence.

He considered lying to her to ease her mind, but realized honesty was smarter. "I doubt if anyone will begin a search tonight." What he didn't tell her was that he doubted anyone would begin a search tomorrow, either. No, he'd save all the gruesome details for later.

"So we're stuck out here for the night." Her voice held a strange tension. It didn't seem to be anger, but rather something deeper, something darker.

"If a search party doesn't show up first thing in the morning, we can probably walk someplace for help." Talbot also didn't mention the fact that he had no idea if he'd be able to walk by morning. His knee throbbed clear down to the bone, and he knew he'd aggravated the old football injury that had, at one time, given him major problems.

"So, all we can do now is sit here in the dark." Again that same tone colored her voice.

Talbot wished for just a spark of light, a tiny illumination that would make her features visible. "I know it isn't going to be the most comfortable night you've ever spent, but there don't seem to be any alternatives."

She didn't speak for a long moment, but he felt the pressure of her shoulder against his. "I don't like the dark," she murmured.

Fear. That was what he heard in her voice, and it astonished him. The cool, always together, always competent Elizabeth McCarthy was scared of the dark. "There's nothing to be afraid of," he said.

He felt her stiffen in protest. "I am not afraid. I just don't like the dark." Still, she didn't inch away from him, but remained with her shoulder firmly touching his.

He didn't believe her protest. She was afraid of the dark. Amazing. One of the things he'd told himself he disliked about her was that she was always in control, always seemed so incredibly strong and efficient.

Someplace deep inside, Talbot had always believed that maybe if she had been a little less strong, a little more needy, then perhaps Richard would have had to mature and accept more responsibility in their marriage.

He found himself wondering what other weaknesses she might possess, and that he entertained any kind of interest in her at all irritated him.

As far as he was concerned, she was the devil in lipstick, a forbidden temptation sent to test his willpower. And yet he couldn't help but be a bit curious. "So how long have you had a phobia about the dark?" he asked.

"It isn't a phobia," she said, then sighed and raked a hand through her hair, causing it to tumble against his shoulder.

He stiffened, fighting the urge to reach up and touch a strand, to see if it was as soft, as silky as it looked. "I think the best thing we can do is get some sleep. I'm sure things will look brighter in the morning."

"Somehow I'm not counting on it," she said softly.

They were the last words they spoke to each other that night.

Talbot tried to make himself comfortable, but the adrenaline that had filled him from the moment he'd realized the plane was going down refused to dissipate enough to allow sleep to overtake him.

He could tell Elizabeth was also having trouble winding down. She squirmed and wriggled next to him, but never allowed her shoulder to stop touching his. As time passed, her wriggling slowed, and he knew she had fallen asleep when her head lolled to his shoulder and she slumped fully against him.

His first instinct was to shove her off him. He didn't want to feel her provocative body warmth against him, didn't want to smell the faint scent of sweet ripened strawberries that wafted from her hair. But he had to admit her body warmth felt good as the night grew chillier.

He closed his eyes, willing his body to relax, knowing it was possible he would need all his wits, all his energy to face the morning.

If they were lucky, they would either be found by somebody who'd seen the plane go down or discover some small town nearby.

If they were incredibly unlucky, they would find themselves in the middle of a forest with nobody around for miles. And the way their luck seemed to be running, that was what worried him.

What if he couldn't walk well enough to find help?

He smiled wryly. Of course, as competent as Elizabeth had always been, she could probably construct a litter from tree branches and pull him out of the forest. This was the last conscious thought he had before sleep finally claimed him.

He awoke with the dawn, for a moment completely disoriented. Before he even opened his eyes, his mind worked to orient him. A warm female form was curled up in his arms, and his nose was filled with the scent of strawberries.

As he drew a deep breath, he remembered. The crash...Elizabeth...the forest. His eyes snapped open and he saw that at some point during the night, their bodies had not only sought the soft, leaf-covered ground, but also each other's.

Her face was turned toward his, and he took the opportunity to study her with the glow of dawn seeping through the trees.

He easily understood why Richard had been so enthralled with her. She was lovely, with sinfully thick lashes and a full, inviting mouth that urged a man to plunder its depths.

Her skin was the color of a barely browned biscuit, with natural peach in either cheek. As he stared at her, his finger itched to caress the skin on her cheek, lightly touch her slightly plump bottom lip.

He wanted her. He'd wanted her for years, and in that desire had been his shame.

Richard's wife. Richard's woman.

With these disturbing thoughts in mind, he disentangled himself from her and sat up. In doing so, he woke her. She stirred and groaned, then sat up and shoved her lioness-colored hair away from her face.

"Ohmigosh. I feel like somebody beat me up all night," she said as she stood and stretched, arms overhead.

Talbot frowned, his gaze drawn to her T-shirt, which had crept up to expose a flat, tanned abdomen. Relief flooded him as she put her hands down and the shirt fell back to where it belonged.

He followed her gaze as she looked around their surroundings and felt her horror as she saw the wreckage that now marred the serene forest floor. She crossed her arms and hugged her shoulders, and he guessed it wasn't the coolness of the morning, but rather the evidence of their close call that caused her to visibly shiver.

"Hard to believe we both walked away, isn't it?" he said.

She nodded, then turned back to look at him. "How's your knee?"

"It'll be all right," he replied, oddly touched that she'd asked.

"Good, because if a search party doesn't show up soon, we may have to hike out of here."

He frowned irritably. He should have known she'd only asked about his knee because she wanted to make sure he didn't hold her back. "We shouldn't do anything too soon. It's just a few minutes after dawn. We'll stay here with the plane for a couple of hours at least."

He could tell she didn't like that idea, that she was ready for action now. And he could guess by the worried frown that marred the smooth skin of her forehead that she was probably thinking of Richard and Andrew.

"They're probably back at your apartment by now," he said as he struggled to his feet. "I'm sure Richard returned to Kansas City when you didn't show up in Twin Oaks last night." His knee screamed in protest as he attempted to put weight on it. He braced himself against a tree.

"You really think so?" The frown that had wrinkled her brow disappeared, and earnest hope shone from those big blue eyes.

Despite her face and clothes being dirty, her hair tangled and decorated with bits of leaves, she looked beautiful. For a brief moment Talbot wanted to take her in his arms, smell that sweet scent that emanated from her and ease away any of her worries by kissing those luscious lips.

The inexplicable tension in Talbot rose to a new

level. "Richard might be a lot of things, but he's always been a good father," he said, his voice sounding harsh even to his own ears.

She stared at him, obviously surprised by his outburst. "You must be hungry," she said. "Richard used to get surly when he was hungry."

He'd expected her to answer his anger with some of her own. Her response momentarily left his speechless. When the ability to speak returned, he eyed her wryly. "I am hungry," he agreed. "Maybe you could forage around in the forest and serve us up a nice breakfast of berries and roots."

She ignored his sarcasm and, instead, eyed what was left of the plane. "If I could find my overnight case—and it survived the fire—I have a bag of corn chips and an apple in it. Surely that would hold us until the search party finds us."

The anger he'd tried so hard to feel, the anger he needed to feel toward her abandoned him. Her gaze once again went to the wreckage wedged between the two trees. "Do you think my suitcase is still there somewhere?"

"I doubt it. If I was to guess, your case is someplace between here and the first place we hit the trees." He shoved himself away from the tree. "We can take a look and see what we find."

She nodded and set off walking at a brisk pace. He stumbled after her, trying to suck up the pain that ripped through his knee with each step. He'd rather suffer than allow her to see any weakness.

They hadn't gone very far when she turned back to him. She stopped walking and placed her hands on her hips. "Sit down," she commanded.

"I'm all right," he protested.

"Yeah, sure. Walking always makes you break out in a sweat." She strode purposefully to where he stood and placed herself under his arm. "I don't want you to blame me when you're permanently crippled because you went chasing after my suitcase," she said as she led him to a tree.

Reluctantly he sat, knowing it was useless to pretend he wasn't in pain. "Maybe if I stay off it a bit longer..." His voice trailed off in frustration.

"I'm perfectly capable of foraging on my own." Once again she set off walking away from him.

Talbot watched her, reluctantly admiring the length of her shapely legs, the slight wiggle of her slender hips. He wasn't surprised that she was handling the situation rather well.

She'd always had the kind of self-confidence that intimidated men. At least, most men. She certainly didn't intimidate him.

He rubbed his knee, realizing that as long as he stayed off it, pain wasn't an issue. Unfortunately there was no doubt in his mind that eventually he was going to have to get up and walk out of here.

As he continued to massage the sides of his kneecap, he frowned, listening to the silence that surrounded him. There was noise—birds called from the tops of trees, and here and there the leaves rustled as squirrels jumped from limb to limb. But these weren't the sounds Talbot most wanted to hear.

What was conspicuously absent was the dull roar of highway traffic, the laughter of a family setting up a campsite. No sounds of human presence at all.

He looked up as Elizabeth came back into view, a triumphant grin on her face and a small battered suitcase in her hand. "I found it!" she announced as she sat down next to him. The case was battered and dented, but appeared to be in one piece. "I looked for your cell phone, but I couldn't find it."

She placed the case on her lap and opened it. Talbot instantly smelled the sweet berry scent emanating from the interior.

The first thing he saw in the opened suitcase was a pair of red lace panties, and his mind instantly produced a vision of her wearing them and nothing else. Heat filled him, and he attempted to shove the vision away.

She quickly buried the panties beneath a mound of innocuous clothing, then grabbed a plastic zippered bag and slammed the case shut.

"I don't know about you, but at the moment a breakfast of corn chips and apple sounds wonderful," she said, her cheeks stained a light pink. "I'm starving."

Talbot was starving, also, but his hunger had nothing to do with a desire for food. It was a hunger he'd suffered for a long time, one that filled him with anger and shame.

He watched as she tore open the bag of chips, then carefully separated them into two piles. "I hope the search party brings water. I have a feeling after eating these chips, we'll both be thirsty," she said.

Talbot knew it was time to tell her the truth, and he dreaded it. So far, she had shown her usual aplomb in the unusual situation. But he wasn't sure how she would react to his little confession. "Uh, about that search party…"

She looked up at him, a chip midway to her mouth. "Yes?" Her eyes narrowed.

"I'm guessing there isn't one."

"What do you mean? Of course there'll be a search party. Doesn't the FAA send people out when a plane disappears? Wouldn't the airport where we were going to land send word that we didn't get there?"

"I wasn't flying into an airport. I was using a friend's airstrip, and I was flying VFR."

"What does that mean?" Her eyes narrowed even more.

"It means 'visual flight rules.' I was not under FAA control or supervision, but rather, my own."

"Gee, why doesn't that surprise me?" she said dryly.

She nudged his share of the corn chips toward him. "You'd better eat up. You're going to need all your strength to help me drag your butt out of these woods."

As she and Talbot finished the last of the apple and chips, Elizabeth fought myriad emotions. She was angry with him for not filing a flight plan, for not taking precautions. How utterly like him to assume he could control, could handle the entire world all on his own.

However, Elizabeth knew not to give in to the emotional pulls, knew that a lot of energy could be wasted being angry. And she needed every ounce of energy she had to get them out of these damn woods.

"You ready?" she asked when they'd finished eating.

"You're angry with me." He struggled to his feet.

"Don't be ridiculous," Elizabeth scoffed. "What makes you think I'm angry?"

"You have a little twitch next to your right eyebrow. I've noticed it before when you're mad."

Elizabeth reached up and touched her eyebrow. She started to protest, then changed her mind. "Okay, maybe I'm a little bit irritated," she confessed.

"Don't you ever vent?" he asked, more than a

touch of irritation in his own voice. "When you get angry, don't you ever scream and rage, throw things and curse?"

"What would be the point?" Elizabeth snapped her suitcase closed and also stood. "Ranting and raving never solved anything. I learned very early in life that venting only gets you into trouble. Besides, you should talk. I've never seen you lose your cool. I always found that annoying about you."

"Let's not start listing the things we find annoying about each other. It would take far too long, and we need to get out of here." He took a step, then grimaced with pain.

Elizabeth once again moved beneath his arm, allowing him to lean on her enough to take some of his weight off his injured knee. Instantly she felt the warmth of his body transferring to her, an oddly intimate sensation that set her frayed nerves further on edge.

"Which way should we go?" she asked him, trying to ignore that, despite an escape from a plane crash and a night spent in the woods, he still smelled good.

He frowned and gazed around them, then pointed in the direction of the wrecked plane. "I think we should go that way," he said.

"Are you sure?" Elizabeth asked.

"Hell no, I'm not sure, but it's my best guess," he replied, his voice containing a surly edge.

"Fine," Elizabeth retorted. "And getting grouchy isn't going to make your knee feel any better or make a rescue team suddenly appear."

"Let's just go," he said, but this time his voice held only weary resignation.

They took off walking, Elizabeth supporting him as much as possible. It was slow going, and neither of them made any effort to talk.

The trees were close together, the underbrush thick and tangled. Squirrels jumped from tree to tree, chattering their anger at the intruders in their domain.

Elizabeth tried to focus on their surroundings, but Talbot's nearness was overwhelming. His arm was around her and his body was pressed against hers as they made their way through the forest, and the strength and firmness of his body somehow didn't surprise her.

She'd always secretly admired Talbot's broad shoulders, slim hips and the stomach that held not one ounce of fat. She wondered what it would be like to be held in his strong arms, not in an effort to help him walk, but held tightly against him in a moment of desire.

She stumbled over a half-exposed thick vine and gasped as Talbot caught her and steadied her against his impossibly firm chest. "Are you all right?" His breath was warm against the top of her head, and she stepped away from him as if he'd breathed fire into her hair.

"I'm fine." She drew a deep, steadying breath. "Why don't we take a break?"

"Sounds good to me," he readily agreed, and together they sank to the ground facing each other.

"How's your knee?" she asked. She wanted, needed conversation to take her mind off the feel of his chest against her own.

"Sore," he confessed.

She frowned thoughtfully. "I hope you aren't doing further damage by walking on it."

"I don't have much choice." He frowned and raked a hand through his hair. Elizabeth noticed the dark stubble that shadowed his cheeks and chin, a growth of whiskers that merely added to his attractiveness. "I'm sorry, Elizabeth. About all of this."

She gazed at him in surprise, waiting for a cutting remark, a touch of sarcasm, a subtle indication that somehow everything that happened was her fault. There was none of those things. His eyes showed genuine contrition.

"There's nothing to apologize for." She pulled her knees up to her chest and wrapped her arms around them, still looking at him. "You didn't crash your plane on purpose, right?"

"Right, but I do intend to have a conversation with my mechanic." The hard glitter in his eyes made her grateful she didn't have the responsibility of maintaining Talbot's plane.

"So, tell me about Twin Oaks. Why did Richard want to take Andrew there so badly? Why did he want me to meet him there?"

Talbot leaned back against a tree and extended his legs in front of him. "I can only guess what Richard thinks by the conversation we had before he left. I told you, the last week or so he's been pretty introspective, and when he does talk, it's been about Twin Oaks. Twin Oaks was the place of our childhood, a time in our lives when everything seemed wonderfully right."

Elizabeth leaned forward, captured by his words, by the very idea of a childhood where everything seemed "wonderfully right" when her own childhood had been so horrifically wrong. "Tell me about it," she urged.

His features relaxed and a smile curved his lips, letting her know his memories were pleasant ones. "Twin Oaks is so tiny it doesn't even warrant a dot on a map. We lived there until we moved to Morning View, Kansas. That was a year before our mom and dad's deaths. Twin Oaks is the kind of town where everyone knows everyone else and there're lots of potluck dinners and town gatherings."

"Sounds lovely." And what was even lovelier than his words was the warmth that emanated from his smile. She'd never before bathed in the warmth of Talbot's smile, and it was a distinctly pleasant experience.

"It was," he said. "I remember it as the only time in my life when I was carefree, and the biggest responsibility I had was going to school." His smile widened and his eyes lit with humor. "And my biggest worry was if Mom was going to make another of her terrible surprise casseroles for dinner."

Elizabeth gazed at him thoughtfully, suddenly realizing the burden that had been placed on him by his parents' untimely death. "It must have been hard for you to be twenty-one and suddenly responsible for a fourteen-year-old."

He shrugged, the smile gone. "The way I saw it at the time there wasn't any choice. I became responsible for Richard, or I let him become a ward of the state and go into foster care. He's my brother and I could never allow that to happen."

He got to his feet. "We should get moving," he said, and in his words she heard him slam the door to any discussion about his past.

Still, as they continued to walk, Elizabeth found herself thinking about the twenty-one-year-old Talbot taking on the role of parent for his younger brother.

When most young people were exploring their first real breath of freedom and adulthood, going to clubs and dating, Talbot had taken the reins of his father's company and accepted the responsibility for a teenage brother. For the first time ever, she felt a grudging respect and admiration for Talbot.

"Are you sure we aren't walking in circles?" she asked after another hour or so. They'd once again stopped to rest.

"I've been watching the sun and I'm pretty sure we aren't." He rubbed his knee thoughtfully. "But I'm surprised we haven't come across anyone, not even a group of campers."

Elizabeth looked up at the waning sunlight that broke through the trees, then looked back at Talbot. "We're going to be here overnight again, aren't we."

"At this point it's a strong possibility." He frowned and raked a hand through his disheveled hair. "It's going to get dark soon, and I don't want us stumbling around in the woods then."

Elizabeth fought the sense of unease that always permeated her when she thought of the dark. "I'm starving," she said in an effort to change the subject.

"Yeah, me too. I'd love a big juicy steak, medium rare, and a baked potato smothered in sour cream." He looked at her with a touch of humor. "And I suppose if your dream meal were in front of you, it would be a lettuce leaf with a drizzle of dressing."

"A lot you know," she retorted. "My dream meal would be a double cheeseburger with a side of French fries and the biggest chocolate shake in the world." She picked a dried leaf from her hair.

"Why on earth would you think I'd be interested in rabbit food?"

"Because whenever you and Richard came to my place for dinner, you usually didn't eat much of anything."

Elizabeth well remembered those nights when she and Richard had first been married and Talbot would request their presence at dinner. How she had hated those family gatherings! "I was always too nervous to eat," she confessed.

He eyed her in surprise. "Nervous? You always appeared amazingly cool and collected to me."

"I was a good actress," she replied. "Inside I was a quivering bundle of nerves and knew if I tried to eat, I'd probably throw up." She grinned at him. "Remember the Big Burger down the street from your house? I used to make Richard stop there on the way home and I'd get a burger, fries and a shake."

She could tell he was surprised by her confession. "What made you so nervous?" he asked.

She hesitated a moment before replying. She couldn't very well tell him that *he* made her nervous, with his gorgeous dark eyes and sculpted features. She couldn't tell him that whenever she was around him, all she could think about was how it might feel if he kissed her, made love to her. At the time, she hadn't even wanted to admit what she felt to herself.

She wasn't about to tell him that her nervousness

and tension around him was a result of an acute awareness of him, not as a brother-in-law, but as a virile handsome man whose eyes constantly held the chill of dislike.

"You," she finally replied. At his puzzled look, she said, "Oh, come on Talbot, I knew how much you hated me. I knew you thought I'd gotten pregnant on purpose in order to trap Richard."

"Why did you marry him?" His eyes held a genuine bewilderment.

"It wasn't just because I was pregnant," she said defensively. "And I certainly wasn't looking to cash in on the McCarthy fortune, even though I knew that's what you believed." She raised her chin, like a prizefighter anticipating a blow. "I was seventeen years old and I thought I loved Richard."

"You and Richard were both far too young to know about love."

"Try telling that to two hormone-driven teenagers," she said dryly. In all the years of her marriage and in the years since her divorce, she and Talbot had never spent any time together alone and had certainly never discussed her marriage to his brother and subsequent divorce.

She frowned thoughtfully, her mind flitting back in time. "I was desperate to belong somewhere. Richard was handsome and fun and seemed to want all the same things I wanted. I desperately wanted to believe that we could build something together. A family.''

She wanted, needed Talbot to understand. She reached out and touched his arm. "Haven't you ever felt passionate about something, about someone?"

"At the moment I'm feeling pretty passionate about getting out of here." He rose to his feet. "We'd better keep moving in what little daylight is left."

He limped off under his own steam, and Elizabeth hurried to catch up. She'd wanted him to understand what forces had initially pulled her toward Richard and ultimately what forces had driven them apart. But it was obvious he didn't care to know.

As she stared at his broad back, she realized he hadn't answered her question. He'd probably never felt passion for anyone, she thought. He'd always struck her as a man who would never understand passion, or love or need.

He'd always appeared strong in his isolation, content with his aloneness. What she didn't understand was why this knowledge of him created a strange ache inside her.

Chapter Three

There had only been one thing in his adult life that had inspired passion in Talbot. To his utter shame and guilt, that something had been his brother's wife. He'd desired her, but knew he would never, ever follow through on that desire.

Still, even reminding himself of this fact didn't ease the pressure that had been building inside him. And he felt that if they didn't get out of these woods soon, if he didn't get away from her, he might explode. The consequences of such an explosion could be devastating to his brother.

Ever since she'd opened her suitcase and he'd spied those red lace panties, his mind had been filled with tantalizing visions of her wearing them and nothing else.

However, what bothered him more than his visions of a half-naked Elizabeth was the vulnerability he'd seen in her for the very first time.

He'd seen the softness in her eyes as she'd spoken of wanting to belong, and he didn't want to think of Elizabeth as soft. He had seen a strange, wistful light in her gaze when she'd told him that she'd learned early on that venting meant trouble.

He didn't want to think of her as soft and sweet and somehow needy.

They walked until the sunlight had faded and dusk was deepening. "We'd better stop for the night," he finally said, reluctant to give up but knowing it was foolhardy to stumble around in the dark.

Elizabeth sank onto the ground with a weary sigh. "I feel like we're in some kind of demented fairy tale, and our curse is to forever wander and never find our way out of this forest."

Talbot eased down beside her, not looking at her. "I'm sorry, Elizabeth. I can't tell you how sorry I am about all this."

Her features were nearly hidden by the deepening darkness. "That's the second time you've apologized, and I told you before, it isn't necessary. I don't blame you for this mess. I just...I just miss Andrew and hope he isn't terribly worried."

Tears suddenly shimmered in her blue eyes and he saw the slight tremble of her lower lip. With amazement, he realized she was on the verge of crying.

Surely not. Not Elizabeth. His mind rejected the very idea of her crying. He'd seen her bail Richard out of jail and never shed a tear. He'd watched her in the throes of labor, when Richard had been playing basketball with a bunch of buddies and couldn't be reached, and no tears had dampened her eyes.

The luminous shimmer of her tears now affected him deeply. Helplessly he watched as a single tear trekked down her cheek.

"I'm sure Andrew knows you're fine," he said, desperate to say anything that would halt the uncharacteristic tears. "He and Richard are probably back at your place now, playing video games and having a wonderful time. And if I know the two of them, they're probably having way too much fun to worry about us."

"You really think so?" Her eyes shone with the light of hope.

"I'm positive," he said firmly. He sent a prayer heavenward that Richard indeed had Andrew back home and they were both safe and sound. "They've probably ordered a pizza for supper and are scarfing it down. If we cross their mind at all, they're probably wondering if we've been abducted by aliens."

To his relief, the tears disappeared from her eyes and she laughed. "I'm sure you're right," she said.

As with the night before, a large tree trunk served

as a backrest as they settled in for the long night ahead. And as with the night before, as the shadows deepened, eventually disappearing into complete and total darkness, Elizabeth inched close to Talbot, so close he was enveloped in her warmth, her scent.

Both played havoc with his senses, stirring him in a way that was both wonderful and terrible. He steeled himself against the sensual assault, hating himself for wanting her…hating her for making him want her.

He leaned his head back against the tree and closed his eyes, wondering what in hell he'd done in his life to deserve the current situation.

Even though Richard and Elizabeth were no longer married, Talbot knew that pursuing any kind of relationship with her was out of the question. The whole thing would feel just…wrong.

Besides, for all he knew Richard had been plotting a way to get Elizabeth back all week, to reunite the family he'd lost. Talbot would never get in the way of a family.

As always, thoughts of Richard filled him with a combination of emotions. Love and protectiveness battled with worry and the vague sense that he hadn't done enough, hadn't *been* enough to make Richard a mature, well-adjusted man.

"Want to know why I'm afraid of the dark?" Elizabeth broke the silence.

He wanted to tell her no, to say that the last thing

he wanted was an invitation into the secret places of her soul. And yet he couldn't help the curiosity that ripped through him. "Okay. Why?"

"When I was five, my parents went out for the evening and left me with a baby-sitter. That night, while I slept, my parents were killed in a car accident." She paused a moment and drew a deep breath.

"I was awakened by a stranger taking me from my bed and was driven to a foster home. When I woke up the next morning, everything I had known and loved was gone. Somehow in my mind, that night the darkness of it and incredible loss became hopelessly entangled."

Although her words had been spoken matter-of-factly, Talbot heard the undertone of profound sadness, the whisper of residual fear.

Despite his resolve to the contrary, it was impossible for him not to be moved. He knew what it was like to lie in the shadows of night and be afraid of what morning might bring. However, when his parents had died, he'd been old enough to hang on to his home, their belongings and his own sense of identity. She had not been.

Unable to stop the impulse that drove him, he placed his arm around her shoulder and pulled her more firmly against him. She pressed her face against the front of his shirt, and he knew her eyes were squeezed tightly shut against the darkness that surrounded them.

"You're safe for the night," he said softly against the sweet fragrance of her hair. "Just go to sleep and tomorrow we'll get out of here."

A helpless resignation swept through him, and he found himself wondering how somebody who was so wrong for him could feel so right in his arms.

They found the motel after awaking and walking for an hour. Elizabeth wanted to fall to the ground and weep in gratitude. She was exhausted and hungry and felt as if she'd never be clean again.

She sank to a bench just outside the motel office as Talbot went inside to see about rooms. He'd been quiet since awaking, refusing to be drawn into any conversation she'd attempted. She'd finally given up, deciding she was as tired of him as he obviously was of her.

The morning sun was warm on her face, and she tilted her head back and closed her eyes, trying not to think about awaking in Talbot's arms.

She'd awoken before he had and been surprised to find herself draped across his chest, his arms circling her and their legs tangled. She had remained in his arms for a long time as he continued to sleep, enjoying the tactile pleasure of his body.

It had been a very long time since she'd awoken in a man's arms. Long before their divorce a year ago, she and Richard had stopped seeking the comfort of each other's embrace.

Talbot's heartbeat had been strong and reassuring against her own, and for a moment Elizabeth had closed her eyes and been able to imagine they were in a clean bed, with silky sheets, and they had just made exquisite love.

She jumped up, cheeks burning from her imaginings, as Talbot exited the office, two keys in hand. "You're in room 104. I'm in 110," he said as he handed her a key. "We'll shower and get something to eat, then decide how we're going to get back to Kansas City. When you're finished cleaning up, come to my room and we'll figure out our next step."

She nodded and they parted ways. As soon as Elizabeth entered the small, tidy room, she spied the phone on the desk. Eagerly she hurried to it, dialed for an outside line, then dialed her home phone number.

Her heart thundered with anxiety as she waited for the phone to be answered on the other end of the line.

"Hello?"

At the sound of the familiar voice, Elizabeth gripped the phone more tightly, relief flooding through her. "Andrew, honey, it's Mom."

"Mom! Where are you? Me and Dad have been so worried! We waited and waited for you to come to Twin Oaks, and when you didn't come, we came back home.''

Elizabeth was so grateful to hear his voice she didn't even take the time to correct his grammar. ''It's a long story, sweetheart, but I'll be home sometime this evening.''

She didn't care if she had to hitchhike back, she didn't intend to spend another night away from her son. ''Are you doing okay? Is your father there? Is he taking good care of you?''

''Yeah, Mom, we're fine. I saw where Dad lived when he was little and the swimming hole him and Uncle Talbot used to go to, and a whole bunch of stuff. Where are you?''

''I'll explain everything when I get there,'' she replied. ''Can I talk to your dad?''

''Yeah, hang on.''

There was a moment of silence, then Richard's voice came over the line. ''Elizabeth, are you all right? Where are you? Is Talbot with you? We've been worried sick.''

''We're fine. Talbot is with me and I'll explain everything later this evening. Wait there for us, Richard. Don't go anywhere until I get home.''

''But where are you?'' he asked.

She briefly explained what had happened.

''This is all my fault,'' Richard said mournfully when she'd finished. ''You're mad at me, aren't you?''

"No, I'm not mad. You couldn't have known the plane was going to crash."

"Yeah, but you're mad about me picking up Andrew without asking you first."

Elizabeth sighed wearily. "We'll deal with that later, Richard. At the moment, I don't have the energy. We should be back sometime this evening and we'll talk then."

She hung up and headed for the shower, relieved that Andrew was okay and confident Richard could handle his son until she got home.

Moments later, she stood beneath a hot, but sporadic spray, soaping liberally with the tiny bar of soap the motel provided.

She sudsed her hair twice, then rinsed it thoroughly, but remained standing beneath the water, enjoying its sensuous heat. Her mind strayed. She imagined Talbot's fingers stroking her body, shooting flames of desire through her—

The soap slid from her fingers and thunked to the floor of the tub. What on earth was she thinking? Apparently the days and nights in the woods had done something dreadful to her brain.

She shut off the water and reached for one of the thin, white towels. She didn't want to think about Talbot, and she certainly didn't want to envision his long, strong fingers dancing over her skin.

She dried herself briskly, wishing she could rid herself of thoughts of Talbot as effectively as she banished the moisture from her skin. But he refused to be exiled from her mind.

She'd fallen asleep in his arms the night before and slept without dreams, without fears, reassured by his strength. But it was more than the mere memory of that strength that now caused her heart to beat a little more rapidly, her body temperature to raise by what felt like several degrees.

She had always known she suffered a strong physical attraction to Talbot, but that attraction had been tempered by the fact that she'd been a married woman. A woman married to Talbot's brother. She wanted to dislike Talbot, knew it would be a defense against the crazy feelings roaring through her.

But it was difficult to sustain dislike when you'd slept in a man's arms, learned nuances of his personality you'd never known before, seen a glimmer of his vulnerabilities.

Dressing quickly, she gave a prayer of thanks that her overnight case contained a clean pair of jogging pants and T-shirt.

By the time she'd brushed her hair almost dry and added a touch of lipstick, she felt back in control, and inappropriate thoughts of Talbot were tucked firmly away. All she wanted was something to eat and a fast ride back to Kansas City and her son.

She grabbed her overnight case and left the room, then went in search of room 110. When she found it, she knocked loudly. The door opened, and all her inappropriate thoughts concerning Talbot came crashing back.

It was obvious he'd just gotten out of the shower. Crisp new blue jeans rode low on his lean hips, and his bare chest displayed sinewy muscle and a liberal sprinkling of dark curly hair.

His hair was slicked back and half his face was covered with shaving cream. He motioned her inside, then headed back to the bathroom. "Have a seat. I'll be with you in a minute."

Elizabeth felt as if she didn't breathe until the bathroom door closed and he was no longer in her vision. Every molecule of air in the room smelled of him, a crisp, clean masculine scent that stirred her senses.

She sat down at the small round table in the corner of the room, trying to dispel the evocative image of his broad chest, his flat abdomen and those lean hips. Dressed, Talbot McCarthy was sharp and stylish and coolly attractive. Half-dressed, he was sexy and hot and definitely dangerous.

What was happening to her? What on earth was wrong with her that she couldn't get these thoughts out of her head? He was her ex-brother-in-law, for goodness' sake, a man who had been cold and distant during the course of her marriage to his brother.

She breathed a sigh of relief when he left the bathroom, his bare chest now covered with a pristine T-shirt. "Where did you get the clean clothes?" she asked, seeking any conversation that would settle her jumpy insides.

"The owner of the motel sent his son to run a few errands for me. Right now he's arranging for a rental car, and he should be here any moment with our meals."

Elizabeth shook her head in amazement. "You certainly know how to get things done."

He smiled a lazy half smile that once again made her tummy buck and jump. "Get me out of the woods and I'm fine. In civilization, money always gets things done."

A knock sounded on the door, and he opened it to a young man who held a paper bag and twin plastic-foam boxes that emitted wonderful smells.

Hunger. That was what made her stomach feel so funny, she thought. It had nothing to do with Talbot's sex appeal.

Talbot thanked the man, then set the items on the table. He opened the bag first and handed her a chocolate shake and removed a soda for himself. When he opened one box and she saw the thick cheeseburger and French fries, she wanted to cry. Not because she was starving, but because he'd remembered what she'd said she wanted when they'd been lost.

She wondered how badly she'd misjudged Talbot in the past. She had always believed him to be a cold, unfeeling man who had exacerbated Richard's problems by picking him up again and again and never letting him fall to the ground. Had she been wrong about him?

"Thank you." She smiled. "How is your leg feeling?"

"Better. The hot shower worked out some of the soreness. I'm sure it'll be fine. How's your head."

"It's fine," she said as she touched the side of her head. "I called home. Richard and Andrew are there and seem to be okay." She popped a fry into her mouth.

"I told you they would be."

"Andrew was bubbling about all the things Richard had shown him in Twin Oaks. Something about a swimming hole?"

A smile flashed across his face. "It was actually a pond. Walter North's pond." He paused to take a bite of his burger and chewed, his smile lingering. "It was the biggest pond in the area, and on most hot days half the kids in town would find their way there, much to Walter's consternation."

"He didn't like you swimming in his pond?"

"Anytime he'd catch us, he'd chase us with his shotgun. But it was a game for all of us."

"A game?" She tried not to notice how achingly handsome he looked with a smile curving his lips.

"He never chased us off in the middle of a hot afternoon. It was always around dusk when he'd come out of his house, acting like he'd just seen us."

Talbot took a drink of his soda, then laughed. "God, what fun it was. Walter was as skinny as his shotgun. He'd cuss and wave his gun and we'd all scream and yell and scramble out of the water."

Elizabeth leaned forward, as if by closer proximity she could feel some of the warmth of his happy memories. She had never considered Talbot a warm, personable man before, but the smile on his lips and the humor that lit his dark gray eyes caused heat to spiral through her.

"I think it was as much a game for Walter as it was for us. He'd never chase us very fast, and I'd lay odds the gun wasn't loaded. Richard was younger than the rest of us and couldn't run as fast, so he'd throw himself at me and I'd run with him hanging on to my back and screaming into my ear."

His smile fell away and was replaced by a deep frown. "That's enough inane chatter. We'd better eat up and get on the road."

They ate in silence and within an hour they were in an economy rental heading back to Kansas City.

Elizabeth tried to focus on the scenery flashing by them, but her thoughts, her entire awareness, were fixed solely on Talbot and the time they had spent together.

She wished, in those two days, she'd discovered

him to be every bit as cold, as dictatorial, as arrogant as she'd once believed him to be.

Shooting him a surreptitious glance, she sensed the power that radiated from him, the strength. She'd always known he was a man comfortable with himself, a man who appeared to need nobody.

Elizabeth had always prided herself on the fact that she needed nobody. She'd once believed she needed Richard, but had quickly discovered that need was tremendously overrated and the people you believed you needed inevitably let you down.

In the past couple of days, she wished she'd found Talbot emotionally deficient and physically repugnant. Once again she directed her gaze out the window and sighed.

She didn't need anyone, especially not Talbot McCarthy, her ex-brother-in-law. But damn him. Damn him for making her want him.

Chapter Four

Talbot tried to focus on the road, but it was difficult when the sunshine streaming in through the windshield stroked rich highlights into Elizabeth's hair and the memory of her slender body pressed against his through the night played in his mind.

Was she wearing those red panties, with the lace riding high on her hips? He could easily imagine the scarlet wisp of lace against her lightly tanned skin.

He gripped the steering wheel more tightly and stepped harder on the gas pedal, eager to get back and put this entire experience behind him.

He would drop Elizabeth at her apartment, then head to the family home in Morning View, Kansas. Once he was back in his own house, surrounded by his own things and busy with the business of running McCarthy Industries, he would quickly forget these three days with Elizabeth.

Surely he would forget how her body fit perfectly against his, how her eyes looked sexy and darkened when she first awakened. Surely he would quickly forget the scent of her hair, the fragrance that seemed to be as much a part of her as her blue eyes.

Hearing the reasons for her fear of the dark had opened up a dimension of her he'd never realized, a vulnerability he wished she hadn't shared with him.

The death of his parents, the virtual demise of his own family, had left a gaping hole in Talbot's heart, and he'd yet to meet the woman he thought might help fill that hole. One thing he knew for certain, it could never be Elizabeth, especially if Richard had been contemplating reconciliation.

He glanced at her again. She was so beautiful with her dainty features and that luxuriant hair. She looked delicate, but Talbot knew that her physical appearance was deceptive. She was emotionally stronger than any woman he'd ever known.

"Why did you stay with Richard for so long? You must have realized in the first couple of months, the first year, that things weren't going to work out between the two of you," he said.

She frowned. "I was young, and I was pregnant with Richard's child. At first I thought he'd change, mature. I thought eventually there would come a time when I would be more important to him than his buddies, when he'd work toward a future, instead of living in the moment." She paused. "I knew the odds were against us from the very beginning because both of us were so young, but I desperately wanted it to work for us."

"But you stayed for so long. Nine years."

She looked out the windshield and didn't answer for a long moment. "I tried, Talbot. I kept thinking there would come a time when I'd have a husband and a child, instead of feeling as if I had two children. That time just didn't come."

"I always admired your strength."

Her gaze met his, and in those blue depths, he saw surprise and a small glimmer of gratitude.

She laughed, and the deep, throaty sound filled the interior of the car. Talbot realized how rarely in their past he'd heard her laugh.

"I don't know whether it's strength or stupidity and more than my share of stubbornness." She raked a hand through her hair, causing it to ripple across her shoulder.

Her smile faded and once again the tiny wrinkle appeared on her forehead. "Talbot, I told you the other night that I grew up in foster care. I had some terrific foster parents and some not-so-terrific foster families, but in my entire youth, there was never any sense of permanence or family."

Again she raked her hand through her hair, lifting

the cascade of honey-colored silk. "When I got pregnant, I swore to myself that my child would have the family I hadn't had—a mother and a father and perhaps a few siblings. The death of that dream was the most difficult thing I've ever had to face."

He nodded and redirected his attention to his driving. He wondered what thoughts whirled around in her head. Did she still love Richard? Did she regret leaving him? If Richard wanted reconciliation, would she agree to it? Would she be willing to give him a second chance to find the happiness she'd once sought?

He dismissed his musings, knowing it was really none of his business what she thought or felt. She was his ex-sister-in-law, and their only real tie anymore was her son, his nephew.

Still, suddenly Talbot wanted the frown on her forehead to be gone. He wanted to hear her laugh again, see her eyes sparkle and shine. A heavy pall had fallen over the conversation, and he searched his mind for a way to lighten things up.

"It wasn't all bad," she said, as if she'd read his mind and was also attempting to lighten the mood. She flashed him a smile. "Remember the picnic we had for Andrew's third birthday?"

He felt the answering smile that curved his lips. It had been a magical day. The weather had cooperated, providing one of those early-spring days where not a hint of winter lingered and the air smelled of the promise of summer. The food had been delicious, Andrew had been charming, as only a three-year-old can be, and Richard had played the role of father and husband beautifully.

"What was the name of your date that day?" she asked, her eyes twinkling wickedly. "Cinnamon? Sugar?"

"Honey," he replied, although he knew she probably remembered the name very well. He laughed and shook his head wryly.

"She was quite stunning."

He nodded. "Yes, she was."

Elizabeth's smile grew more wicked. "And she was so innovative in her dress for a picnic. Who would have thought of wearing spike heels, a leather miniskirt and a bustier to a birthday party for a three-year-old?"

"She's the only woman I've ever met who thought pâté was the bald spot on top of an old man's head."

He was rewarded with her laughter. Rich and throaty, it filled the car, and he joined in as each memory called on another one of that crazy, glorious day.

"Every time she leaned over to look at the cake, I was afraid her, uh, assets might spill out," Elizabeth continued.

Talbot laughed again. "I don't know what was

worse, her bending over to look at the cake or trying to play Frisbee in those shoes.''

"She might not have been overly bright, but I'm sure she had a good heart,'' Elizabeth defended her.

"No, she didn't,'' he protested. "She thought children were 'yucky' and animals were dirty and believed a humanitarian award should go to Coco Chanel for finally coming up with clothing that women with breasts could wear.''

"Still, it was a nice party, wasn't it? Did you date her much after that day?''

"That was my first and last date with the lovely Honey. I liked her fine until she talked, and unfortunately the lovely Honey loved to talk.''

Elizabeth laughed again, then sobered and he could feel her gaze on him. "Why haven't you married, Talbot?''

Because the woman I wanted was already taken by my brother. He shoved the unwanted thought aside. "I don't know. I've been so busy building the business, I haven't taken much time for romance. Besides, I think I'm probably best alone.''

"Nobody is best alone,'' she protested softly.

He glanced at her sharply. "What about you? Why haven't you remarried?''

She emitted a dry laugh. "Who has time? Besides, I'm not alone. I have Andrew. Between work and all of Andrew's activities, I meet myself coming and going.''

Talbot focused on the road again. They had reached the city limits of Kansas City, and traffic had become thick. He wanted to protest, to tell her that a son wasn't the same as a man in her life.

Instead, they both fell silent as Talbot battled the traffic, tried to concentrate on his driving and not on Elizabeth.

With the women Talbot had dated in the past, he'd always found that familiarity did, indeed, breed contempt. But with Elizabeth, it seemed to be breeding something quite different.

The car accident his parents had when he'd been twenty-one had stolen his mother's life instantly, but his father had lingered for two long days in the hospital. "Promise me," he had said as Talbot gripped his hand and begged him to fight for life. "Promise me you'll always take care of Richard. He's not strong like you."

And Talbot had promised. Even before his parents' deaths, there had been times when Talbot felt more like Richard's father than a brother.

As Talbot wheeled into the apartment complex where Elizabeth lived, he pushed aside thoughts of the past.

He pulled up before her building and stopped the engine, surprised by the vague sense of disappointment that seeped through him. "Guess the adventure is over," he said.

"Yeah, guess so." For a moment, he thought he

heard the same disappointment he felt in her voice. "Are you coming inside?"

"No. I need to get home, and you need to talk to Richard." He got out of the car as she did the same. He grabbed her suitcase from the back seat and handed it to her, then walked with her partway to her door.

"Thanks for taking care of me, Talbot," she said.

He smiled. "I didn't take care of you. If you were in the woods by yourself for a week, my bet would be on you."

"Still, it was nice not to be alone...to have somebody with me during the darkness." A slight blush stained her cheeks, and God help him, he wanted to reach out and stroke her skin.

It was an ache deep within him, the need to touch her one last time. "Just tell Richard I'll see him back in Morning View." He bent forward to give her a perfunctory kiss on the cheek.

He wasn't sure what happened—whether he aimed wrong or she turned her head at the last moment—but suddenly his lips were on hers.

The kiss was no more than the mere touching of lips, but Elizabeth felt the power of the intimate connection right down to her toes. His mouth, which always appeared rather stern and forbidding, was in reality soft and sensual and filled with heat.

However, before she had time to respond in any

way, he released her, turned on his heel and stalked away.

As Elizabeth watched him get into the car, she raised a trembling hand to her lips where the imprint of his mouth felt like a brand.

He'd kissed her. Talbot McCarthy had kissed her. Why on earth had he done it? What had prompted him to kiss her?

His car pulled out of the parking area and disappeared from sight. She stared after it for a long moment, trying to make sense of what had just happened.

She turned to go into her apartment, confusion whirling inside her. The kiss had been so unexpected. And what confused her more than anything was the knowledge that someplace deep inside her, she'd wanted him to kiss her, again and again.

Andrew greeted her at the door, banishing any other thoughts from her head. He gave her an exuberant hug, and for a long moment Elizabeth clung to her son, grateful that everything had turned out well and everyone was all right.

"Elizabeth, I'm so glad you're okay," Richard said as he rose from the sofa. "Where's Talbot?"

"He headed on to Morning View," she replied. "He said he'd see you there." Elizabeth looked at the man she had married so long ago.

Richard wasn't as striking or as potently male as his brother, but he was a pleasantly handsome man, with warm brown eyes that had always sparkled with boyish enthusiasm and a mischievous glint. At the moment neither the glint nor the spark was apparent. His eyes held a somberness Elizabeth had never seen before.

"Dad made pot roast," Andrew said. "With carrots and potatoes."

"He did?" Elizabeth looked at Richard in surprise. "I didn't know you knew how to do a roast."

Richard shrugged. "Andrew can't eat junk food all the time when he's with me. It isn't good for him."

Elizabeth stared at him, wondering when a pod person had replaced Richard. The man she'd known for the past ten years had never worried about the effects of junk food on himself or his son.

"That sounds marvelous," she finally said, and realized the meal with Talbot had been hours ago and she was hungry again.

"It's ready when you are," Richard replied.

"Just let me go wash up and I'll be ready." Elizabeth went into the bathroom. Richard had cooked a pot roast and Talbot had kissed her. This had to be the strangest day of her life.

For a moment she stared at her reflection in the mirror, surprised to find her lips weren't swollen or red. There was no lingering indication of Talbot's kiss other than the burning memory of his mouth against hers.

She sluiced her face with water, hoping the cool liquid would banish the heat of that memory, the taste of him. Why had he kissed her? And, more importantly, why had she wanted him to?

The moment had obviously been one of those anomalies of nature, an uncharacteristic act between two people who had shared an unusual or life-threatening situation. She'd heard of such things— people making love in the midst of disaster, kissing strangers when a stressful situation was over.

They had narrowly escaped death when the plane had gone down, had shared two nights and days together, lost in the woods. Reaching the apartment complex had indicated an end to the drama, and surely that was what had prompted the kiss. It had really meant nothing to him, and she certainly didn't intend to make anything of it.

She dried her face, then left the bathroom and went into the kitchen where Andrew and Richard were already seated at the table.

The dinner conversation remained pleasant and light. Andrew told her everything they had seen while in the tiny town of Twin Oaks. When he mentioned the swimming hole again, he added, "Dad said sometimes they would go skinny-dipping!"

Elizabeth fought the image that filled her mind— that of a naked, dripping-wet Talbot emerging from a sparkling pond.

"That must have been the pond where the farmer

would chase you with a shotgun," she said to Richard.

"Really?" Andrew looked from his mother to his father.

Richard looked at her in surprise. "Talbot must have told you that."

"There isn't a lot to do other than talk when you're lost in the woods for two days," she explained.

Funny, she thought as they continued the meal, she'd confessed to Talbot her fear of the dark, something she'd never told anyone before, something she hadn't even shared with the man she'd been married to for nine years.

She focused her attention back on Andrew, who was now telling her about seeing the house where his father had lived as a young boy.

Elizabeth knew the McCarthys had lived in Twin Oaks until Talbot was twenty and Richard thirteen.

At the time, their father was making more money than any of them had ever imagined from his small computer business, and the family had built a dream mansion in Morning View, Kansas, and moved in.

The family had lived there only a year before Keith and Maggie McCarthy were tragically killed on the way home from a business trip, leaving behind a thriving business and two sons to pick up the pieces.

It wasn't until much later, after the dinner dishes

had been washed and put away and Andrew was in bed, that Elizabeth and Richard sat at the table with cups of coffee to talk.

"You've been unusually quiet," Elizabeth observed. "Is something on your mind?"

Richard twirled his spoon in his coffee to dissolve the sugar he'd added, a small frown creasing his broad forehead. "Actually, I do have something to talk to you about." He set his spoon down, leaned back and sighed.

A wave of apprehension swept through Elizabeth. She'd never seen Richard this way, so somber, so serious. "What is it, Richard? What's going on?"

He seemed to consider his words carefully before speaking. "For the last couple of months, I've been having problems with headaches and dizziness and blurred vision. I thought maybe I needed glasses, so I went to an eye doctor, but he didn't find anything wrong."

Elizabeth's apprehension increased as he broke his gaze from hers and picked up his spoon to stir his coffee yet again. She noticed his fingers trembled slightly, and the spoon clattered once again to the table.

"Richard, you're scaring me," she said, and reached out to take his hand in hers. "Just tell me straight out. What's going on?"

"I have a tumor."

The words hung in the air, and for a moment Elizabeth prayed desperately that she'd misunderstood them. "A tumor?" she echoed faintly as his fingers squeezed hers tightly.

"A brain tumor."

Elizabeth now didn't know if it was his fingers trembling or her own. Emotion welled up inside her, filling her throat and stinging her eyes. She willed it away, knowing that Richard would draw his strength from hers.

It had always been like that between them. Elizabeth held Richard together, and when he did fall apart, she had always been the one to put the pieces back together.

She swallowed hard, seeking and finding control. "Have you told Talbot?"

He shook his head. "Not yet. I'll talk to him when I get back home tonight."

"Okay." She pulled her hand from his, swallowed again to clear away her emotion and straightened her shoulders. "Okay, you have a brain tumor. So, what's the prognosis?"

"If I don't do anything...eventually it will probably kill me." Richard got up from his chair, as if he was unable to sit still another moment. He paced the floor in front of her for a minute, then stopped and looked at her.

In the depths of his eyes, she saw his fear, and a fear of her own swept through her. Despite the divorce, in spite of the fact that Richard could never be the right man for Elizabeth and he had caused her a wealth of tears throughout their marriage, she cared about him.

He shared a big piece of her past, was the father of her son and, for these reasons alone, would always own a tiny section of her heart.

"The doctor wants to do surgery," Richard said. "According to him, the tumor is in a place where he is fairly confident he can get it all."

"Then you'll have the surgery," Elizabeth said with a matter-of-factness she didn't feel.

"Easy for you to say. They aren't talking about cutting into your head."

"It doesn't sound to me like you have any other option," she replied. She stood and walked over to him. Again she reached for his hand. "Richard, you have to do what the doctor says is for the best. If you don't do it for yourself, then do it for Andrew. He needs you as his father, and he's going to continue to need you for a very long time to come."

"Yeah, some father I've been." His voice held a heavy dose of self-condemnation.

"You've always been a good father," she protested.

He grinned, knowing she was being generous. His grin was a flash of something comfortable and familiar. "I'm a good father when I take the time to remember I'm a father."

She nodded, a lump growing large in her throat. "And that's why you have to have the surgery."

"I know." He stepped away from her. "And I'm going to have it. I've done a lot of thinking since getting the diagnosis." Again he flashed his boyish smile. "There's nothing like a little brain tumor for making a person reevaluate his priorities."

His smile faded. "I haven't spent enough time with Andrew. I haven't told him so many things I want him to know, important things that only a father can tell a son. I suddenly feel like I don't have any time left."

"You have years and years left," Elizabeth said fervently.

"I won't lie to you, Elizabeth. I'm scared."

She fought the impulse to wrap him in her arms. She could offer him her strength, but knew Richard would ultimately have to find a well of strength within himself to meet the challenge ahead.

"You're going to have that surgery, and they are going to get every bit of that tumor. You're going to teach Andrew how to drive a car, and tell him all about girls, and be there when he makes you a grandfather."

He nodded, and studied her for a long moment. "I have a favor to ask you. I want Andrew to come and stay with me and Talbot in Morning View for the next couple of weeks."

A protest formed on Elizabeth's lips, but Richard

held up a hand. "I want you there, too. I know Andrew hasn't really spent enough time alone with me to be comfortable without you around for that length of time. I want some time with my family before I go into surgery."

"Oh, Richard. I don't think that's such a good idea—"

"Please, Elizabeth. It would mean so much to me."

His gaze bore into hers, and she'd never felt so torn. She wanted to be there for Richard, not because she loved him as a woman loves a man, but rather as a dear friend. He was Andrew's father, and she wanted to support him, be there for him.

And yet...her mouth still burned from the fire of Talbot's unexpected kiss, and the thought of staying in the McCarthy home with the two brothers caused her head to throb with tension.

"Don't answer right now," Richard said. "I know you've been through a trauma of your own, and I've dumped a lot of stuff on you. I'll head back to Morning View now and call you tomorrow."

She walked with him to the front door, her mind reeling with all the sensations, all the emotions the past three days had wrought.

She knew she was on sensory overload, and when Richard left, she leaned against the door and fought the tears that threatened to overwhelm her.

"Mom?" Andrew appeared in the hallway.

"Honey, what are you doing still awake?" Elizabeth pushed herself away from the door and shooed her son back into his bedroom. "It's getting late, and you have school in the morning."

He climbed back into bed and she tucked the sheet around him. "Dad told me about his tumor when you weren't here," Andrew said. "He explained to me about the operation he's got to have, and I heard him talking about us staying with him and Uncle Talbot for a while before he has the operation. Can we do it, Mom?"

The words tumbled from him one right after another, and finally he closed his mouth, but his eyes spoke more eloquently than words. His eyes were so like Richard's, a soft brown that radiated his emotions.

"I don't know, Andrew. You've got school and I've got work. I don't see how it's possible for us to just pick up and leave for a couple of weeks."

"But, Mom, Dad is sick. He needs us."

Andrew's words ripped through her. Richard *was* sick, and more than anything he wanted the support and love of his family. Wanted them around him. How could she deny him? How could she deny her son this time with his father?

She reached out and stroked Andrew's dark hair. He was the spitting image of his father, although even at nine, Andrew had a maturity and inner strength that often awed Elizabeth.

"I'm not going to make any decision tonight," she finally said. "I'm really tired and I need to think things through with a clear mind."

"Okay, but I really think we should do it, Mom. I think we should do it for Dad."

Elizabeth kissed him on the forehead and wished him good-night, then left his room and went into her own bedroom. A sudden, staggering exhaustion overtook her.

She peeled off her clothes and slipped on the pale-pink cotton nightshirt that was as familiar as a hug from an old friend. She turned out the light, then crawled beneath the covers of her bed with the aid of the night-light that burned in a socket next to her bed.

It was funny. Most children had night-lights in their bedrooms, but in this household it was the mother who needed the illumination to ward off the things that went bump in the night.

However, at the moment it wasn't the night that worried her. Rather, it was the coming of dawn, when she knew she'd have to make a decision.

Richard needed Andrew...and Andrew needed her. Richard was right in that she knew her son wouldn't be comfortable for a couple of weeks away from her.

For the past nine years Richard had been sporadic in his visitations, often canceling at the last moment. Andrew had borne his father's shortcomings good-naturedly, always embracing the time they spent together, but never holding a grudge when plans didn't materialize.

Elizabeth knew if she didn't agree to this time with Richard, Andrew would never forgive her if something horrible happened. And she would never forgive herself.

But there were practical considerations. Andrew had just started in the fourth grade, and although he was an excellent student, missing two weeks of school couldn't be good.

As a substitute teacher, she could take off the next two weeks, although she would be financially pinched. There were so many things to consider.

For the first time in years, she wished she had somebody to hold her through the night, to stroke her back and whisper that everything was going to be just fine. She frowned, irritated by the uncharacteristic yearning.

Rolling onto her back, she stared up at the shadows on the ceiling. Touching her lips, she thought of that moment when Talbot's mouth had claimed hers.

As his lips had touched hers, heat had soared through her, searing her from their point of contact down to the tips of her toes.

She shoved the memory firmly out of her mind. She couldn't think about that kiss, and she couldn't think about Talbot. Thinking about it, thinking about him, filled her with an uncomfortable guilt, and she wasn't sure why.

Closing her eyes, she drifted off to sleep, afraid she'd make the wrong decision and somehow equally afraid she'd make the right one.

eyes were hidden behind her curling lashes. Her soft

Chapter Five

A brain tumor.

Talbot stood at the window in the huge McCarthy kitchen and watched as the sun's first rays peeked over the horizon. His eyes felt gritty as he sipped his coffee. It had been a long, sleepless night.

Richard had arrived home by eleven the night before. Talbot had been in his study, taking care of what business he could that had reached crisis stage during his absence.

After suffering a plane crash and a seemingly endless trek in the woods, Talbot had thought nothing more could shake him. But when his brother had divulged the information about his brain tumor, Talbot felt as if he'd taken a vicious punch to the gut and the world beneath his feet had been suddenly whisked away.

There had been times in the past when Talbot had wanted to knock some sense into Richard, when his brother's careless spontaneity and boyish antics had driven him half-crazy. But nothing in all the years since their parents' death had prepared Talbot for what Richard now faced.

Brain surgery. Talbot knew no matter how many assurances the doctor had given Richard, that kind of surgery was always dangerous.

The two brothers had stayed up for most of the night, talking about the diagnosis, the plan of action, the challenges ahead.

Talbot sighed and moved away from the window to pour himself another cup of coffee.

A damn brain tumor.

And there was nothing Talbot could do to make it better. There was no way to fix the problem for the brother he loved.

He'd only felt this helpless two other times in his life. The first had been that dreadful night in the hospital when he'd held his father's hand, willing him to fight for life, and watched him slip away.

The second time of helplessness had come just the night before—in that insane moment when he'd kissed Elizabeth.

He shook his head, as if the physical action alone could dislodge the memory of the sweet warmth of her lips, the heady scent of her that had momentarily scnt caution and any kind of rational thought scattering to the winds.

While Richard had been digesting his diagnosis and contemplating a fight for his life, Talbot had been wandering in the woods and lusting after Richard's ex-wife. The thought made him feel ill.

He turned at the sound of footsteps approaching the kitchen. A heavyset, gray-haired woman entered, her broad face wreathed in a welcoming smile. "Talbot. It's good to have you home."

"Thanks, Rose. It's good to be back." He sat down at the round oak table, his mug of coffee before him.

"The house is far too quiet when you and Richard are gone." She bustled over to the stove and grabbed an apron from where it hung on a hook. "Scrambled eggs and toast?" she asked as she tied the colorful apron around her.

"Sounds great," he said.

Rose Murphy had worked for the McCarthy brothers since their parents' deaths. Unmarried, and liking it that way, she had embraced the running of the McCarthy home with an efficiency that had made Talbot's life much easier.

Through the years, she'd become not only invaluable as cook and housekeeper, but also as a means of emotional support and advice for Talbot.

Within minutes she'd prepared the eggs and toast

and set the plate before him. She poured herself a cup of coffee and joined him at the table.

"You look tired," she said, her brown eyes bright and sharp as they peered at him.

"I am tired," he confessed. Quickly, between bites, he told her about the plane crash and the days wandering in the woods.

"You must have had an angel on your shoulder!" Rose exclaimed when he'd finished. "You could have died when the plane went down. My heart shudders to even think of how close you came to death."

He nodded. "We were very lucky." He hesitated a moment, then added, "And I sure hope that luck continues to hold."

"Why? You planning another plane crash?"

Again he paused a moment before replying, gathering his thoughts, then told her about Richard and what was ahead for him.

The words came haltingly, and he kept a firm grip on his emotions, refusing to allow them to careen out of control. He had to be strong. He didn't have time for fear or grief. He had to be strong to get through this, for himself, but more importantly, for Richard.

When he'd finished, Rose wiped the tears from her eyes with the hem of her apron.

Like most people who met Richard, Rose adored him. She often complained that he was irresponsible and immature and unreliable, but despite his many faults, Richard garnered affection like flowers drew bees.

"That poor boy," she said softly. She wiped her eyes one more time, then straightened in the chair. "We'll all have to do whatever we can to help him fight this thing. Richard isn't strong, but we'll have to help him be strong."

"That's exactly what we need to do," Talbot agreed.

He finished his meal, then left the kitchen and headed for his office. He closed the double doors behind him and sat at the massive desk.

The room was huge, with floor-to-ceiling bookshelves on one wall and an elegant built-in bar on the other. The entire house had been his mother and father's dream, a six-bedroom mansion that was an oddity in the tiny town of Morning View.

The home base of McCarthy Industries was housed in a large building twenty minutes away in Topeka, Kansas. With the invention of the telephone, the fax machine and the computer, Talbot was able to conduct much of the business of McCarthy Industries from right here in his home.

At the moment, the last thing Talbot felt like doing was working. He picked up the paperweight that sat on the desk. It was an ugly thing, a globe of glass with a dollar bill inside.

His mother had had it made for his father in the

early days of McCarthy Industries, when the "office" was at the kitchen table and the breeze through the open windows blew papers everywhere.

As Talbot held the globe in his hand, he thought of his father and the promise he'd made to him. "I promise I'll take care of Richard."

And he had done his best in the past fourteen years to fulfill that promise. He'd tried to give Richard everything he believed his parents would have wanted. Besides the tangible things, he'd tried to guide, support and impart wisdom to his younger brother.

He had cared for Richard through his rebellious teen years, had tried to be there for him when he'd become a young father. Talbot had done everything in his power to take care of Richard, but there was nothing he could now do to make everything okay for the brother he loved.

Placing the paperweight back on the desk, he stared at the phone. Last night Richard had told Talbot his wishes concerning spending time with Andrew before the operation.

He explained that he'd voiced his wish to Elizabeth, but she had been reluctant. Richard had begged Talbot to get Elizabeth and Andrew here for a couple of weeks, and Talbot had agreed to do what he could.

He looked at his wristwatch and realized it was still too early to make any calls. He might as well get some work done while he waited for a more appropriate time.

An hour and a half later, Talbot picked up the phone and hit the speed-dial number that would connect him. The phone on the other end rang three times, and he wondered if she'd taken a job for the day. He knew she substitute taught and had been taking classes at night to finish her degree.

She picked up on the fourth ring.

"Hello." Her familiar voice filled the line, and Talbot gripped the phone more tightly in an effort to ward off any feelings, any sensations that might surface inside him.

"Elizabeth, it's me."

There was a moment of silence, then a soft, "Hi."

"We need to talk."

"Richard told you?"

"Last night."

Again a moment of strained quiet. "I guess none of us got much sleep last night," she finally said.

"We need to discuss you and Andrew coming here to stay for a couple of weeks." He didn't want to make small talk with her, needed to get their business conducted as quickly as possible.

Her sigh was audible. "I just don't know what to do. I want to do the right thing...."

"We all want to do the right thing."

"But there are so many things to consider. Andrew is in school and then there's my work."

"I'll hire a tutor to work with him every day. We'll make sure he doesn't fall behind. And as for your work, I've already made arrangements for your rent and utilities to be paid for the next month. If you need additional funds, I'll see that you get them."

"I don't want you to do that," she protested. "I don't want you to pay for anything."

"Elizabeth, now is not the time to stand on pride. I know how financially difficult it will be for you to take that much time off, but this is more important than money."

She was silent for long moments. "Of course you're right." She sighed again. "We'll come, but I'm not promising we'll stay for two weeks. Surely Richard needs to get in to have the surgery as soon as possible, and it shouldn't be that long."

"That's true," Talbot agreed evenly. "But you know how difficult it can be to change Richard's mind once he has something in his head. So, we can expect you sometime this evening?"

"No, we'll leave tomorrow morning. That will give me some time to make arrangements and get us packed. You can expect us around noon." Her voice was brisk and businesslike.

"That will be fine. Richard will be pleased."

They said their goodbyes and hung up. Talbot reared back in his chair and rubbed the center of his forehead, where the beginnings of a headache tapped an irritating dance.

He was thankful she hadn't mentioned their time spent together. More, he was profoundly grateful she hadn't brought up the brief kiss they'd shared. She had been as cool and collected as he had been, and that was exactly how it had to remain between them.

It was all about Richard. Richard's health, Richard's well-being, Richard's happiness. Richard wanted to spend some time with Elizabeth and Andrew, and that was the way it would be.

This was a big house, and Talbot worked long hours here in his office. It was possible they would see very little of each other during the next couple of weeks. And that was just fine with him.

He rubbed his forehead again, realizing his headache was intensifying. He knew it was the right thing for Elizabeth and Andrew to be here. But as he thought of her silky soft hair, the bright hue of her eyes and the sweet curve of her lips, he knew he'd just invited temptation into his home.

Morning View, Kansas, was a charming small town with a Main Street reminiscent of years gone by. There was an ice-cream parlor, a café, a general store and sundry other shops that spoke of a slower pace of living and the warmth of a close community.

It had been a full year since Elizabeth had been in Morning View. At that time she and Richard had been living out the last gasps of their marriage in an apartment building on the outskirts of town. Although Andrew spent weekends occasionally with his dad, who now lived back in the family home, this was Elizabeth's first trip back since the divorce.

Andrew squirmed with excitement in the passenger seat, pointing out places he'd gone with his father as if she was a first-time visitor to the area.

He giggled as he pointed to the ice-cream parlor. "One time Dad and I went in there and ordered an ice-cream cake and we ate the whole thing for dinner."

Elizabeth shook her head ruefully. How like Richard.

"It was really good, but I had a tummy ache all night," he added.

"Gee, I wonder why," Elizabeth said. Andrew grinned at her, then looked back out the window.

"I like it here," Andrew said. "And it's going to be so cool for all of us to be together in the same house."

Elizabeth frowned. She didn't know how "cool" it was going to be, but she intended to make the best of the situation for Richard's sake. And for Andrew's.

They drove through the town, then took a two-lane road for half a mile. There, on the right, sitting on a large hill, was the McCarthy mansion.

A white, two-story house sporting a sweeping

front porch and huge columns, the place resembled a Southern plantation more than a Midwest farmhouse. It was imposing in its grandeur, and Talbot had always seemed to belong here with his cool disdain and touch of arrogance. The lord of the manor and the king of his world.

She needed to think of him as cool and arrogant and not particularly likable. She had to believe that about him in order to get through the next few weeks of living in his home, being in his immediate presence.

She definitely needed to forget the Talbot she'd been in the woods with, the one who had displayed a sense of humor, who had held her through the darkness of the night. The one who had kissed her and made her burn from head to toe.

She parked in front of the house on the circular drive. Before she and Andrew could exit the car, Richard bounded out of the house, radiating energy, his face lit with a huge grin.

"You're here!" he said as Andrew got out of the car. He ruffled his son's hair, then pulled him into a quick embrace. "Your room is all ready for you, and I put your mom in the room next to yours."

"Cool," Andrew replied. "Where's Uncle Talbot?"

"Holed up in his office where he is most of the time." Richard smiled at Elizabeth. "Well, come on. Let's get you unloaded and settled in."

Between the three of them, they managed to get all of the things from Elizabeth's car in one trip. They put Andrew's suitcase in his room, then dropped Elizabeth's in the room next door. A bathroom joined the two rooms.

"Talbot's room is down the hall on the left, and mine is on the right," Richard explained to her. "You know if you need anything, all you have to do is ask."

"I'm sure we'll be fine," Elizabeth told him.

"Have you guys had lunch? I thought I'd take us into town to the café." He looked from Elizabeth to Andrew.

She knew it was time to lay some ground rules. These days were about Richard and Andrew, not about the three of them spending time together. She didn't want to confuse Andrew in any way, didn't want him to start to think that maybe this was the beginning of the three of them being a family again.

She loved Richard, but not in the way a wife loves a husband. She could never be married to him again. "Why don't you and Andrew go? Is Rose still here?" When Richard nodded, she continued. "I'd love to have some time just to sit and visit with her."

"Okay," Richard agreed easily. "Ready, partner?"

"Ready," Andrew replied, and the two of them

hurried down the hallway with barely a backward look.

Elizabeth sighed in relief. Richard's easy acceptance lay to rest her concerns about his motives for inviting her here. It was really only to make Andrew more comfortable.

The room Richard had put her in was attractive, done in soft pastel colors that instantly soothed her. She walked over to the window and pulled aside the peach-colored gossamer curtains to peer out.

From her vantage point, she had a perfect view of the nearby stable and the corral area. Several horses were in the pasture, their tails flicking as they dipped their heads to the lush grass.

A soothing room and soothing scenery. So why did she feel as if all the nerves in her body were stretched taut. Why was her stomach so twisted in knots? She refused to consider what the answer might be.

She left the room and headed for the kitchen. The minute she stepped into the large, cheerful room, she found herself in Rose's warm embrace.

"Oh, mercy, it's been too long!" Rose declared. "Let me look at you." She held Elizabeth at arm's length, her brown eyes warm and welcoming. "Ah, just as lovely as ever."

"I've missed you, too." Elizabeth gave the old woman one last hug.

"Sit down," Rose commanded. "I was just about

to fix me a meat-loaf sandwich for lunch. Will you join me?''

''I'd love to.'' Elizabeth slid into a chair at the table and watched as Rose prepared the two sandwiches. She and Rose had gotten close during the first year of Elizabeth's marriage.

At seventeen, Elizabeth had known little about cooking and caring for a household. She'd often called Rose for the recipes of Richard's favorite foods and tips on keeping house. And in those phone calls, the two women had developed a friendship.

But, as often happened with divorces and changes, when Elizabeth had moved to Kansas City, the two had lost touch.

''I was going to make a sandwich for Talbot, but he left to go into Topeka just before you got here,'' Rose explained as she set plates on the table. ''I guess work piled up while you two were lost in the woods.'' She shook her head ruefully. ''You were mighty lucky to escape with your lives.''

''Don't remind me,'' Elizabeth replied with a wry grin. ''I've never been so scared in my life as the moment when Talbot said we were going down.''

As the two ate lunch, they chatted about everything from new stores in town to the people Elizabeth had known when she'd lived here.

They spoke of Andrew, whom Rose adored. ''He's got his father's looks and energy, and thankfully your good sense to temper it,'' she said.

The stress Elizabeth had momentarily felt upon arriving melted away beneath the warmth of Rose's smile and the easy conversation between them.

This won't be so bad, she thought. She'd been worried about having to spend too much time around Talbot, but odds were good that they would rarely see each other in the weeks ahead. He had his work, and she had brought a handful of books to read.

Besides, she was an adult, and she'd spent ten years of her life fighting the attraction she felt for him. She could continue to fight the attraction for another couple of weeks.

Once Richard's surgery was behind him and he was on the mend, they would return with their usual visitations, and Elizabeth would have no reason to interact with Talbot. As long as she didn't think about that kiss, she'd be fine.

When they'd finished lunch, Elizabeth went back upstairs. She didn't want to wander the house, not knowing when Richard and Andrew would return, but more importantly not knowing when Talbot would return.

In Andrew's room, she unpacked his suitcase, putting away clothes in the closet and drawers, then setting out the items he'd thrown into the suitcase, items he claimed he couldn't live without.

A baseball cap and a ball, a handheld video game, a sketch pad and his colored pencils, and a woolly bear he insisted he didn't *have* to sleep with, but always did. She lined up the items across the top of the dresser, then stepped back and looked at them.

Her son. He was a terrific kid. Easygoing, he rarely pouted or threw fits. Andrew was the one thing Elizabeth and Richard had got right. And although he had easily adjusted to the divorce, adapted to the sporadic visitations with his father, Elizabeth knew the loss of Richard in his life would devastate him.

When she finished unpacking Andrew's things, she went back into her bedroom and started on hers. Noticing a clock radio, she turned it on and found an easy-listening station, then got busy with the music playing softly.

She had brought mostly casual clothing, which she folded neatly and placed in drawers. The two dresses she'd brought, she hung in the closet. Like Andrew, she had packed several things that had nothing to do with clothing.

She'd brought paperback books by favorite authors, several textbooks so she could study for the classes she intended to take next summer. She piled these on the nightstand and moved her hips to the beat of the rhythmic music.

"Elizabeth."

She gasped and whirled around to see Talbot standing in the doorway. "Talbot!" A blush warmed her cheeks. "How long have you been there?"

"Long enough to know you obviously don't need hip-replacement surgery." One corner of his mouth curved into a smile. Her blush intensified. "I'm glad you and Andrew got here okay."

She nodded. "We arrived about an hour ago." Why was it that the air in a room always seemed to get displaced the moment he appeared?

Had he always been as handsome as he appeared at the moment? Clad in a worn pair of jeans and wearing a black ribbed shirt and a pair of loafers without socks, he looked casual yet elegant and utterly masculine.

"It appears you've fully recovered from our adventure," he said, and his gaze momentarily flickered down the length of her. Heat suffused her in response to his gaze.

"I'm fine. What about you? How's your knee?" Go away, she wanted to scream. Go away. Don't look at me like that. Don't talk to me. Please, make these days here easier on me by staying away from me.

"Still a bit sore, but all right," he replied. "Are you finding everything you need?"

"Everything is fine. We'll be just fine." Her voice sounded higher-pitched than usual.

He stepped closer to her and she realized he held a small paper bag in his hand. "I've made arrangements for a tutor to begin working with Andrew first thing tomorrow morning. He'll work with him from eight to eleven every day while you're here.''

"Thank you.'' Her mouth was uncomfortably dry, and she just wanted him gone.

"I better get back to work,'' he said. "Oh, this is for you, to make your stay here more comfortable.'' He handed her the small paper bag, then turned on his heel. "I'll see you at supper.'' He disappeared from sight and she heard his footsteps carrying him down the hallway.

She drew a deep breath and slowly released it, then sat on the edge of the bed. She'd hoped she would have no reaction to seeing him again. She'd hoped the odd yearnings that had affected her during the course of their three days together had been an anomaly that had nothing to do with reality.

But now she had to face the fact that something drew her to Talbot—the same something that had been at work during the course of her marriage to Richard. Although for the course of her marriage she had remained one hundred percent committed to her husband, she had always been aware of a tension, a chemistry, a desire, at work between her and his brother.

She'd handled it during her married years by rarely placing herself in a position where she had to be around Talbot. And in all those years she had never ever put herself in a position of being alone with him.

Until the plane crash. Until they'd talked for long periods of time, shared tiny pieces of themselves. Until all those crazy feelings had returned with a vengeance.

This is about Richard, she reminded herself firmly. Richard wanted his family around for support and love. He certainly didn't need his ex-wife lusting after his brother. She was certain that would only add additional tension, additional stress on a man who faced a huge challenge.

Besides, it wasn't as if she loved Talbot. Deciding that whatever it was she felt for him was just some sort of craziness that would pass, she reached into the bag he'd handed her.

Her fingers closed around the object. She pulled it free and stared at it.

A night-light.

It was shaped like a pretty flower with a hummingbird drinking from the center. Talbot had bought her a night-light.

Her heart contracted in a way that nearly evoked tears of wonder as she continued to stare at the unexpected, thoughtful gift.

He would have had no way of knowing she always packed a night-light with her, that she would never risk leaving home to stay in a strange place where the night might be too dark.

He had remembered her fear and gone out and bought her a night-light.

As she plugged the light into a socket near the bed, she wondered if in agreeing to come here, she hadn't made the biggest mistake of her life.

Chapter Six

"**M**om, get up!"

Andrew bounced on her bed with the enthusiasm of a natural early riser. Elizabeth groaned and tried to burrow deeper beneath the blankets. "I've been up for an hour, and Rose let me help her make biscuits. She said to tell you breakfast will be ready in about twenty minutes."

Elizabeth rolled over on her back and squinted open an eye to look at her son. He was already dressed, and besides his blue jeans and red sweatshirt, he wore a bright, eager smile that gladdened her heart.

"Do I really have to get up?"

"Yes!" He grabbed her by the hand and tried to pull her from the bed.

She laughingly gave in. "Okay, okay, I'm getting up!"

Andrew jumped off her bed and headed for the door. "Now I'm going to go wake up Dad," he announced, and hurried away.

Elizabeth grinned, knowing there was only one person in the world who hated getting up early more than she—and that was Richard.

She remained in bed for another few moments, then got up and padded into the bathroom. She covered a yawn with the back of one hand as she turned on the water for a shower.

She felt as if she could sleep another ten hours and knew it was because she had slept so restlessly the previous night. She quickly stepped into the shower and tilted her head up to meet the warm spray.

Talbot had not joined them for supper last night. It had been just the three of them. After dinner, Richard and Andrew had gone for a walk, and Elizabeth had returned to her room, not wanting to accidentally bump into the man who spent far too much time in her thoughts.

When she'd finally gone to bed, the night-light he'd bought for her had cast a reassuring glow not only in the room, but in her heart.

As she dried herself, she steeled herself for whatever the day ahead might hold. If she tried to spend every minute of every day in the bedroom, by the end of her visit she would be completely insane. She had to get out a little, even if it meant running into Talbot.

Moments later, dressed for the day in a pair of jeans and a navy sweatshirt, she headed downstairs for the kitchen. Before she reached the bottom of the staircase, she heard the sound of male laughter coming from the kitchen.

It was easy to identify the high-pitched giggles of her son, the uninhibited laughter of Richard and the low-pitched rumble from Talbot.

"Ah, there she is," Richard said as she entered the kitchen. "Sit down." He pointed to the chair between him and Talbot. "It's all on the table."

"I'm sorry if I kept you waiting," she said as she slid into her chair. Beneath the smells of fried bacon and buttery, baked biscuits, she could detect the familiar fragrance of Talbot's aftershave.

"Did you sleep well?" Talbot asked.

"Yes," she replied, although it wasn't true. "Thanks," she added softly, knowing he would know what she was thanking him for.

He nodded and averted his gaze.

"We were just having a discussion on who can make the best pizza," Richard said. "I say it's me."

Andrew rolled his eyes and grinned at his mother. "I told Dad I could probably make a better pizza than him. The last time he tried to make me pizza, he burned the crust black. Besides, he makes his from a box.''

"That's because we started playing catch in the yard, and I forgot all about it baking,'' Richard protested. "And what's wrong with a box?''

"You all know I'm the master pizza maker around here,'' Talbot said, joining in the fun. "Several pizzerias in different cities around the world are always trying to buy my old family recipe.'' His dark eyes glittered with humor and his lips curved into a smile.

That smile. That killer smile that was so rarely used, and yet, whenever she saw it, her heartbeat became just a little faster than normal. She suddenly felt as if the air was too thin to breathe and quickly busied herself by buttering one of the flaky, golden biscuits.

"Really?'' Andrew asked dubiously.

"Andrew, your Uncle Talbot is full of baloney,'' Richard said with a laugh. "Besides, if his recipe was an old family recipe, I'd have it, too.''

"I have never been full of baloney,'' Talbot protested. "I don't even like baloney.''

Andrew giggled with delight at the good-natured banter.

"It sounds to me like there's only one way to settle the matter,'' Elizabeth said, finding their high spirits contagious, despite her unease.

"And what's that?'' Richard asked.

"A pizza bake-off. Right here in this kitchen to-night." The three males stared at her, then slowly they all began to smile.

"I'm in," Richard said.

"Me, too," Andrew said.

"I wouldn't miss it for the world," Talbot said with a lazy grin. "And Elizabeth will be the judge."

Elizabeth laughed. "I must warn you all. I'm a tough pizza critic."

"The tougher, the better," Richard said enthusi-astically.

"But if we win, what do we win?" Andrew asked. "There has to be a prize or something if it's going to be a real contest."

"I'll pick up something in town," Elizabeth of-fered. "I'll get something really special. And I'll be happy to do any grocery shopping that needs to be done for the big event. Just make me a list, each of you, of what you need to create a masterpiece pizza. I can make the trip into town this morning while Andrew is with his tutor."

Andrew made a face, indicating what he thought of the tutoring deal. "I think it would be more ed-ucational to go to town with you."

Elizabeth laughed. "Nice try, kid."

"I'll take the ride with you," Richard said. "If you don't mind, there're a few things I need to take care of."

''That's fine,'' she agreed hurriedly, grateful it wasn't Talbot who had offered to go with her.

Throughout breakfast, she was far too conscious of Talbot. She tried not to notice how he seemed to possess not only the chair he sat on, but also the immediate space surrounding it.

Even in the mere act of eating, he appeared powerful and in control. Sexy. Twice their legs brushed under the table, and each time Elizabeth jerked away as if she'd encountered fire.

Fortunately Richard and Andrew provided entertainment and conversation, and the details of the pizza contest were hashed out, making the meal pass swiftly.

Immediately upon finishing his meal, Talbot excused himself and left the kitchen, and Elizabeth found herself relaxing.

When the rest of them were finished eating, Rose appeared to clear the table and shooed away any offers from Elizabeth to help.

Elizabeth was on her way back to her bedroom when Talbot appeared at the bottom of the stairs. ''The tutor is here. I thought you might want to meet him.''

She nodded and followed him into his office. As she walked behind him, she couldn't help but notice how his shoulders filled out and stretched the material of his T-shirt. His jeans fit him as if they'd been made exclusively for him, molding to his slim hips and well-shaped buttocks.

Lordy, she was having problems thinking of him as a man she'd never really liked, a man who had intimidated her and been cool and distant with her throughout her marriage to Richard.

All she seemed to be able to think about was those strong arms holding her through the dark, scary night, of his lips lightly pressed against hers in a kiss she'd wanted to go on...and on.

In the office a pleasant-looking, sandy-haired young man sat in a chair before the large desk. He stood as they entered the room.

"Elizabeth, this is Todd Green. He comes highly recommended and with impeccable references," Talbot said.

"Hi, Todd." She held out her hand, and the young man gripped it firmly. She wasn't sure whose hands were sweaty, Todd's or hers.

"How do you do," he replied. "I'm looking forward to working with your son. Mr. McCarthy has told me he's a great kid."

Elizabeth flashed a quick smile at Talbot, then looked back at Todd. "He *is* a great kid, and I'm sure the two of you will work very well together."

"I'm ready to get started whenever he is," Todd said.

"I thought I'd let them work in here where they won't be disturbed," Talbot explained.

Elizabeth frowned. "But what about your work?"

"I don't plan on doing a lot over the next couple of weeks. If problems arise at the company, I have responsible men in charge who will call me."

Elizabeth nodded, oddly disturbed by the knowledge that he didn't intend to work during the time she and Andrew were in the house. Somehow this knowledge made Richard's condition more frighteningly real than it already was.

"I'll go find Andrew so you can get started," she said to Todd, then turned and left the office.

It had been almost easy to look on this time in the McCarthy household as a vacation of sorts. But Talbot never took vacations. He'd always been obsessed about the family business and controlling his life with precise efficiency. He rarely took time off for anything or anyone.

It wasn't until Andrew was in the office with Todd that Elizabeth and Richard left to drive into town for groceries.

"Thanks, Elizabeth," Richard said as they pulled away from the house.

"Thanks for what?" she asked.

"For letting this happen. For coming here and letting me spend extra time with Andrew." He stared out the passenger window for a long moment. "I want— I need to make memories for him...just in case something goes wrong."

"Nothing is going to go wrong," Elizabeth said firmly. "I refuse to consider any other outcome."

Richard laughed, and she cast him a quick glance. "What's so funny?" she asked.

"Me, you. When we were married, one of the things that drove me crazy about you was your strength. I always got the feeling that you were fine if I was there, and just as fine if I wasn't. You always had things under control, no matter how much chaos I brought into our house."

Elizabeth didn't know how to reply, wasn't sure what he expected her to say. In any case, he gave her no opportunity to reply, but instead, continued. "Your strength, which I couldn't handle in our marriage, is now what I need from you. I need you to believe that everything is going to be okay, and I need you to make me believe that, too."

"You know I'll do whatever I can to help you get through this, Richard," she promised.

She tightened her grip on the steering wheel. He had no idea just how strong she would have to be in order to put aside the craziness she felt when she was around Talbot. It was a craziness of wanting Talbot to kiss her again, then utter madness of wanting Talbot to kiss her again, the utter madness of wanting Talbot to hold her not just for a minute, not just for an hour, but through the rest of the nights left to her on earth.

* * *

A pizza bake-off. He must have been out of his mind to agree to such a thing. Talbot stood in his office peering out the window where Richard and Andrew were playing catch. He knew Elizabeth was upstairs, waiting for the contest that would take place in a little while.

As he stared at his brother, his mind flashed over the years that he'd tried to be a parent to him. There had been a lot of laughter in those years—and a lot of tears.

Richard had been more than a handful, and Talbot had spent many a sleepless night wondering if he was doing too much or too little to guide his brother through adolescence and into well-adjusted, responsible adulthood.

Richard had never been a particularly demonstrative child, not given to easy displays of affection. But as Talbot watched his brother and his nephew play catch, he noticed how often Richard breached the distance between them and give his son a clap on the shoulder or a quick hug. It was as if Richard was trying to store up a lifetime of touches and hugs in case something went wrong during the surgery.

He'd noticed during the infrequent visits with Elizabeth and Richard during their marriage that the two of them rarely touched. He'd never seen his brother plant an absent kiss on Elizabeth's forehead, stroke her back unconsciously or take her hand while they walked.

Talbot would find it impossible not to be a toucher with Elizabeth. If she belonged to him, he'd want to touch her silky hair every chance he got, run his fingers down her smooth cheek, put his arm around her slender shoulders.

But she doesn't belong to you, a small voice reminded him. She belongs to Richard. Family ties still bind her to him and will forever make her off-limits.

He turned away from the window as Richard and Andrew finished playing catch and ran toward the house. The loneliness that had plagued Talbot in the past several years hit him square in the heart. He sank down behind his desk and leaned back in the chair.

Surely the feelings he was experiencing for Elizabeth had to do with the fact that he'd been without a woman in his life for a very long time. Before Richard's surprising marriage to Elizabeth, there hadn't been time for Talbot to maintain any sort of relationship with a woman. Richard and the business had sucked him dry every minute of every day.

After Richard had married and moved into town with Elizabeth, Talbot had dated off and on, though he'd never found a woman with whom he could imagine spending the rest of his life.

Casual movie dates, occasional dinners, a variety of women passing in and out of his life, but nobody who had touched him profoundly. Nobody who had managed to ease the loneliness that had become his constant companion.

Of course he would have strong feelings for Elizabeth. She was beautiful and sexy and here in his home, here where he smelled her sweet fragrance in every room, felt her very presence. But for all he knew, he'd be having these same feelings for any woman who was temporarily staying in his house.

This thought made him feel better.

"Uncle Talbot?" Andrew called through the office door. "It's time to make pizza."

"Okay, I'm coming," Talbot replied. He stood and steeled himself for the night to come, a night that he knew would be filled with laughter, family, fun—and Elizabeth.

"Mom!" Andrew hollered up the stairs. "Come on."

Elizabeth and Talbot met at the kitchen door, where Andrew stood as sentry. "Welcome to Mc-Carthy Pizzeria," Andrew said with a studied soberness that the dancing light in his eyes belied. He led them through the doorway.

The kitchen had been transformed. A red-and-white checkered cloth covered the surface of the table, and a candle burned brightly in its perch atop an empty wine bottle. Soft music played in the background, and Talbot recognized Dean Martin singing something in Italian.

"I will show you to your table, Madam Judge,"

Andrew said, offering her his arm in gentlemanly fashion.

"Thank you, sir. I've heard that the pizza here is world-renowned." It was obvious she intended to throw herself fully into her son's game.

Suddenly that was what Talbot wanted, as well. A night of laughter, of fun, with no thoughts of the past, no worries about the future.

He grabbed Rose's apron from the hook next to the stove and wrapped it around him with a flourish. "And of course, I am the master chef of this establishment." He flicked his fingers toward Andrew and Richard. "And these are my rather dull students attempting, in vain of course, to best me at my specialty."

Richard hooted his derision and Andrew giggled. "We will see who is the true master when the contest is over. Let the baking begin."

Elizabeth had shopped to make the contest as even as possible. At their separate workspaces on the countertop, each had a package of pizza-crust mix, a large jar of sauce and a dozen toppings to use at his discretion. They were allowed to use any spices in the cabinet, and they each had a pizza stone to prepare their creation on.

Talbot was acutely aware of Elizabeth seated at the table, sipping a glass of red wine. Clad in a pair of rust-colored slacks and a blouse to match, she looked like a beautiful autumn leaf blown into the kitchen. He frowned, pulling his gaze from her and to the work at hand.

"Hey, Andrew, did you know that a crushed, flat box can sail over tall grass as fast as a sled can slide over snow?" Richard asked.

"Really?"

Richard nodded. "When we lived in Twin Oaks, your uncle Talbot and his buddies used to race down a big hill on crushed boxes. Remember that, Talbot?"

Talbot grinned as he covered his ball of crust to allow it to rise for a few minutes. He turned around and smiled at his brother. "I remember. And if I recall, you insisted on trying it even though we all told you that you were too young."

"And what happened?" Andrew asked.

"Your dad took off like a kite in the wind, flying down the hill. Unfortunately he forgot one little thing."

"What?" Andrew asked eagerly.

"I forgot to watch where I was going," Richard replied. "I flew right off that hill and into a pond. I sank to the bottom like my rear end was filled with stones. Your Uncle Talbot had to jump in and save me."

"And then I got grounded when we got home, because Richard told Mom and Dad I tried to drown him in the pond," Talbot added.

Richard laughed. "That's true. As Talbot pulled

me out of the water, he called me a pain-in-the-butt twerp, and that made me so mad I got him into trouble.''

This story invoked another, and another, and as they worked, the kitchen filled with laughter and the warmth of family.

Talbot tried to keep his gaze from Elizabeth, but it was impossible. Like a moth drawn to a flame, he was drawn again and again to the laughter in her eyes, the obvious pleasure that lit her features as the stories grew wilder and crazier.

By the time the pizzas were all in the oven, the kitchen looked like a battle zone. Flour splattered every surface, and sauce speckled the top of the stove. Bits of mushrooms, shredded cheese, slices of pepperoni and onion littered the floor, transforming the plain white tile into a kaleidoscope of colors and shapes.

''Rose is going to kill us all,'' Elizabeth said, then took a sip of her second glass of wine. Talbot didn't know if it was the wine or the laughter that filled her cheeks with blossoms of color. In any case it didn't matter. All that mattered was that she looked lovelier than he'd ever seen her.

''It's a good thing I gave her the night off. She'd go crazy if she saw this mess,'' he said.

''Hey, it takes a mess to create masterpieces, right, buddy?'' Richard ruffled Andrew's hair affectionately.

"How long does it take to bake? I'm starving," Andrew said, then picked a piece of pepperoni off the countertop and popped it into his mouth.

Talbot opened the oven door and peered inside. "Just a couple more minutes and they should be ready."

"If I don't eat in a few minutes, I'm going to be tipsy," Elizabeth said, and pushed her wineglass aside. "And if I have the awesome responsibility of judging this contest, I have to have my wits about me."

"You won't need your wits to know that mine is the undisputed best," Richard said, gaining catcalls and boos from his brother and nephew.

Talbot couldn't remember the last time he'd enjoyed an evening more. They had all cut up and acted silly. And the warmth and positive feeling continued as they ate.

"I'm not making any final decision until I've eaten all I want of each pie," Elizabeth announced as she started on the first piece.

They sat around the table, everyone sampling not only the pizza they had baked, but the others, as well. And as they ate, the pleasant talk continued.

"Mrs. Walker in the grocery store said to tell you hi," she said to Talbot. "And that her daughter, Alva May, just got engaged."

Talbot winced. "I dated Alva a couple of times,

and I think her mother had already printed up wedding announcements for us.''

"Why didn't you marry her, Uncle Talbot?" Andrew asked.

Talbot leaned toward the young boy and grinned. "Because she had hairy legs and smelled like a burning tire.''

Andrew snorted soda pop and spewed pizza. Elizabeth burst into peals of laughter, and Richard joined in with his own chuckles.

Talbot continued, "You see, Alva is a mechanic down at Walker's Garage. She's twice my size, and she didn't really love me at all. She just wanted to replace the shocks in my car.''

"You're terrible!" Elizabeth exclaimed.

He held out his hands in a gesture of helplessness. "So shoot me. I don't like hairy legs and the smell of burnt rubber.''

He was grateful when nobody pursued the topic and asked him what he *did* like in a woman. He would have had to answer that he liked a woman who had hair the color of butterscotch pudding and eyes as *bright* blue as gift-wrapping ribbon.

He liked a woman who smelled as fresh as spring rain, as sweet as a summer flower. He even found endearing the tiny dab of sauce that decorated her slightly pointed chin.

"Mom, are you ready to make a decision yet?" Andrew asked anxiously.

Elizabeth smiled and dabbed her face with her napkin, removing all trace of sauce from her chin. "Yes, I think I'm just about ready to announce the winner."

"Before you do, Mom, I want to tell you something." Andrew got up out of his chair and moved to his mother's side. He slid an arm around her neck. "I just wanted to tell you you're the best mom in the whole wide world."

"Hey, no fair buttering up the judge," Talbot protested with a laugh.

"Who, me?" Andrew batted his lashes in innocence. "I just wanted her to know that I love her more than anything."

"If anyone is going to be successful buttering up the judge, it's going to be me," Richard interjected. "After all, I'm the one who might not be here in a couple of weeks."

Elizabeth gasped, and whatever frivolity had been in Talbot's heart blew to shreds beneath the weight of Richard's words.

A roar resounded in his ears—the roar of fear unexplored, of unrealistic rage, of guilt unnamed and of promises unkept.

He stumbled to his feet, wanting, needing to get out, away, before he lost control. As he left the kitchen, he vaguely heard Andrew admonish his father. "Jeez, Dad."

"It was just a joke," Richard said softly.

But the problem, Talbot thought, was that it wasn't a joke. It was a possibility, a distinct possibility he'd refused to face until this very moment.

He raced for his bedroom, needing the familiarity, the privacy of that room, because he knew that for the first time in his life, he was about to lose control.

Chapter Seven

Richard looked at Elizabeth helplessly as Talbot strode out of the room. He was like a contrite young boy who had done something wrong and now needed guidance on how to fix it. "I'm sorry. That was incredibly stupid. I just wasn't thinking," he finally said.

"Maybe you should go to him," Elizabeth suggested, a vision of Talbot's face frozen in her mind. "He looked pretty upset."

Richard appeared terrified at the very idea. "Nah. When Talbot's upset, he always wants some time alone. It's better to let him work it out himself."

"Maybe you and me should go to that movie we were gonna see," Andrew said to his father.

Richard's face lit up. "That's a great idea. And

by the time we get back, I'm sure everything will be fine.''

Before Elizabeth knew it, she found herself alone in the silence and the mess of the kitchen. She sank down at the table and poured herself another glass of wine.

She took a sip and shook her head, marveling in the wake of the chaos Richard had left behind. It felt far too familiar and reminded her of all the reasons their marriage hadn't worked.

Richard had always meant well, but he'd lacked the maturity to form a real commitment to their marriage, a true bond with her. He'd preferred hanging out with his friends, shooting pool and drinking beer. He'd often spoke thoughtlessly, never intending to be hurtful, but succeeding just the same.

She knew he hadn't meant any harm with his remark, that it had simply flown from his lips without first circulating through his brain, but she couldn't get the vision of Talbot out of her head.

When Richard had spoken those words, all color had fled from Talbot's face, and the look in his eyes had painfully pierced her heart.

The man she had always seen as vital and strong, as powerful and in control, had suddenly appeared filled with despair and anguish.

He's an adult, she told herself. He's a grown man. Let him handle this the way he's handled everything else in his life—alone. She took another deep swallow of her wine.

She knew all about alone. From the time her parents died when she'd been a young child, she'd been alone. She knew now her marriage to Richard had been an attempt to assuage the deep loneliness that assailed her, but being married to Richard had made her feel more alone than ever.

Swallowing the last of her wine, she girded herself for the task of cleaning up the incredible mess the three males had made. But thoughts of Talbot made concentrating on anything else impossible.

Did he handle things alone because he wanted to, or because he had no other option? Did he need somebody to talk to? Somebody to share the emotions that must surely be whirling inside him?

Knowing it was the wrong thing to do, but utterly helpless to do anything else, she went in search of him. He wasn't in his office, nor was he in any of the rooms on the ground level of the house.

She climbed the stairs quickly, knowing if she paused to think twice, she'd retrace her footsteps and run back to the kitchen. She had no idea what she intended to say to him once she found him. She only knew she couldn't stand the thought of him alone and in pain.

She found him in his bedroom, standing at the window, almost hidden by the evening shadows that had usurped much of the light of the room. Had his door been closed, she would have never breached his privacy, but the door stood wide open, an unspoken invitation for her to enter.

"Talbot?"

He didn't turn to look at her, and for a moment she wasn't sure he'd heard her.

"Are you okay?" She took a step toward him, fighting the impulse to place her hand on his rigid back, smooth away the tension in muscles she knew were bunched just beneath the surface of his skin. Instead of reaching out to him, she balled her hands into fists at her sides.

"My father lived for two days following the car accident that took my mother's life instantly." His voice was deeper than usual and held the slight tremor of emotions barely contained. Still, he faced away from her and out the window, as if the answers to any questions would be revealed by the coming of the night.

"For those two days he drifted in and out of consciousness. He knew he was dying, and I think he embraced death because he knew my mother was waiting for him. In those two days, he told me he wasn't worried about me or the business. He wasn't worried about the house or things left unfinished. But he was worried about Richard."

Talbot's shoulders rose and fell as he sighed, and again Elizabeth fought her need to touch him, to somehow ease the pain she could hear in his voice.

She moved closer, so close she could reach out and touch him, so close the scent of his aftershave wrapped around her.

"Dad knew Richard could be thoughtless…careless. He wasn't a bad kid, he just didn't think things through, didn't consider the consequences of his actions. Dad made me promise I would always take care of him." He finally turned to look at her, his eyes glittering and haunted. "I don't know how to fix this."

She placed a hand on his arm, felt the tension that knotted his muscles. "You can't be in control of everything, Talbot," she replied.

"But I made a promise, a vow."

She wondered if he recognized the irrationality of his words. "There are some promises that can't be kept no matter how badly you want to keep them," she said softly.

She dropped her hand from his arm, but didn't move away. "Talbot, you've done your job. You have fulfilled your promise to your father. Richard is an adult. You can support him and love him, but you can't carry his burden for him. He's going to have to get strong for himself."

Talbot raked a hand through his hair, then clenched his hands into fists, the tension that radiated from him almost palpable. His eyes seemed unnaturally bright, and she could tell he was fighting for control.

"I'm so angry," he said. "I'm angry and I'm sad and I'm..." He allowed his voice to trail off, but Elizabeth knew what he'd been about to say.

"I'm afraid, too," she said, her voice a mere whisper.

For just a moment, she thought she'd gone too far, invaded his emotions and thoughts too deeply. He glared at her as if nonverbally demanding she take back the words, as if refusing to acknowledge his own fear.

"He's my only brother, the only family I have left." His voice held the deep ache of loss.

"And he's my son's father, the only father Andrew will ever have."

The air in the room was charged, as if lightning was about to strike or an explosion was about to detonate. She saw him fighting the battle for control. And control won.

He sighed, some of the tension leaving him. "I'm sorry if I messed up the pizza party."

"You didn't mess up anything," she replied. "Richard spoke thoughtlessly, and it's only natural that his words would upset everyone."

"Where is he now? Where's Andrew?" He shoved his hands into the pockets of his jeans and leaned back against the window frame.

"They went to a movie."

He shook his head, a rueful half smile forming on

his lips. "Typical. He stirs things up, then makes his escape."

Even his partial smile had the power to send rivulets of warmth through her. She was suddenly aware of the fact that she stood in his bedroom, mere feet from the huge, four-poster bed.

The bed, with its navy-plaid spread and large, fluffy throw pillows seemed to beckon a body to fall in and enjoy. A warning whisper echoed in the deepest recesses of her mind.

"Speaking of things stirred up, I need to get back to the kitchen and deal with the mess. Rose would have a heart attack if she saw the present condition of her kitchen." She needed to get out of this room, get some distance from him.

"I'll help," he said.

"That's not necessary," she protested quickly. "I really don't mind."

"I'll help," he repeated firmly. "I was a party to making the mess, so I'll be a party to the cleanup."

She wanted to protest more strongly, tell him she could do it herself, that his help wasn't necessary. But she couldn't very well tell him to stay out of his own kitchen.

He followed her from his bedroom and down the stairs. She was aware of him with every step she took. She could feel the heat of his gaze on her, sweeping across her shoulders, sliding down the length of her back, lingering on her buttocks. Or was it just her imagination working overtime?

She was grateful when they reached the kitchen and together began to put away food, wiping countertops and filling the sink with dishes that needed to be washed.

Elizabeth wondered how it was possible for a kitchen so large to suddenly feel so small. No matter where she cleaned, Talbot was too close to her, filling her senses with his masculine presence.

"You can tell me the truth while Richard and Andrew aren't here," he said as he filled the sink with soapy water.

"The truth?" She eyed him curiously.

"My pizza was the best." The shadows that had darkened his eyes had lifted, leaving in their wake the self-assurance, the slight edge of arrogance she'd always found so attractive.

She laughed. "To be perfectly honest, they all tasted about the same. Although I must admit yours was certainly the neatest. I could tell just by looking at them whose was whose. Andrew's was loaded with his favorite topping—pepperoni. Richard's was a sloppy mess, and yours had the look of a neat, compulsive overachiever."

She was grateful that he laughed, the rich, deep sound shooting warmth through her.

"What did you get as a prize for the winner?"

he asked as he rolled up his shirtsleeves, then plunged his hands into the soapy dishwater.

"An ice-cream cake decorated like a pizza." She picked up a dish towel and moved next to him, steeling herself against any pleasure that might sweep through her by being so near. "I figured that way everyone could share in the spoils of victory."

"Good idea."

She watched as he rubbed the sponge across a plate. She tried not to notice the strength of his bare forearms, his long, sensual fingers as he scratched at a stubborn splash of sauce. She could almost feel the stroke of those long fingers across her flesh.

He handed her the plate to dry. "In fact, when we finish with the cleanup, I think we deserve a piece of that cake."

"Sounds good to me." Perhaps the ice cream would cool her off, make her stop having inappropriate thoughts about Talbot.

For a few moments, they worked in silence. He washed, she dried, their fingers touching briefly as they passed the dishes from one to the other. Elizabeth wondered if he felt the electric sparks that fired off each time their hands brushed.

He didn't appear to. In truth, he seemed distant, and she found herself wishing she could crawl into his head, see into his thoughts.

"Do you ever worry that you're doing too much

for Andrew?" he asked as the last dish was put away in the cabinet.

"Sure," she replied. "I worry that I'm doing too much. I worry that I'm doing too little. So, you want a piece of the ice-cream cake."

"Definitely. Why don't you get the cake and I'll make some coffee?" he suggested.

Within minutes, they were seated at the table, a steaming cup of coffee and a piece of cake before each of them. "Why did you ask me that about Andrew? Do you think I do too much for him?"

"No, not at all," he said firmly. "You're a terrific mother." He rubbed the rim of his mug with his thumb and frowned thoughtfully. "I just sometimes worry that I didn't do enough, or I did too much, where Richard is concerned."

She smiled. "And you worry that you were too hard on him or too soft. And you worry that you spent too much time with him or too little. Sounds perfectly normal to me."

He nodded and cut into his cake. "I was just wondering if maybe you and I haven't made it really easy for Richard not to be responsible and grown-up."

"What do you mean?" she asked, defensiveness rising inside her. Surely he couldn't blame her for Richard's problems with maturity. She had married a boy—who had remained a boy, in spite of all their years together, all their marital angst.

"Relax," he said. "This isn't an indictment of

your skills as a wife." He took a bite of the cake, then continued, "I was just thinking that both of us suffer from the same condition."

"And what condition would that be?"

"A self-reliance that is perhaps a bit daunting to others." He took another bite of his cake and eyed her. "In all the years of your marriage to Richard, you never once asked for my help. When Richard forgot to pay the electric bill and your service was cut off, you didn't call for help, you simply handled it. You handled a million different crises and never asked me for help."

"I would have cut off my arm before I would have asked you for help."

"And why is that?"

"I knew you didn't approve of our marriage, that you thought we were too young…and I knew you weren't sure at all that you approved of me. Besides, it wasn't your responsibility. I was and always have been accustomed to handling my problems on my own."

She stared down into her coffee mug, unable to tell him the real reason she'd never asked him for help—that she'd been afraid if he ran to her rescue, she would have to face the fact that she'd married the wrong brother.

She'd closed off from him. A moment earlier, her eyes had been windows into her thoughts, allowing him in, but now they were firmly shuttered.

They ate in silence for a few minutes. Again a sweeping range of emotions filled Talbot. He was angry at fate, worried sick about what the future held, and for the first time in his life he was scared to death that he was going to have to face it all alone.

He suddenly wanted Elizabeth back with him. He wanted her to once again be open with him, sharing with him. He reached out and lightly touched the back of her hand. "I've made you angry."

"No," she protested. "I was just thinking about what you said." She ate the last bite of cake, then shoved her plate aside and wrapped her hands around her coffee mug. "Maybe you're right. Maybe I was so used to taking care of myself and my life, I never really gave Richard an opportunity to share in the responsibilities."

"And maybe if you had attempted to make him share more of the responsibilities, he would have run for the hills, because I never gave him the tools to cope with real life."

She smiled, and Talbot reveled in its warmth. She had the prettiest smile he'd ever seen. It lit her from within. "So what is all this? A culpability party? The two of us are responsible for Richard's immaturity and he isn't?"

"No." Talbot returned her smile with one of his own. "No, Richard has to accept his part in who he is—and who he is going to be in the future." If he has a future. Unexpectedly, emotion tore through him again, and he felt the burning press of tears in his eyes.

Aware of Elizabeth's gaze on him, steady and knowing, and aware of an uncharacteristic vulnerability, he jumped up from the table and turned his back on her to rinse his plate.

With the water running in the sink, he didn't hear her approach, didn't know she'd left the table and stood just behind him until he felt the warmth of her hand seeping through his shirt.

"Talbot, you aren't in this all alone. I'm here for you—if you need me."

If he needed her? Heaven help him, right now his need for her positively consumed him. The plate clattered to the stainless-steel bottom of the sink and he whirled around to face her.

In the instant it took for him to reach for her, he knew someplace in the back of his mind that he'd lost control, and he didn't even attempt to gain it back.

Before she had time to protest, before he gave himself an opportunity to think, he wrapped her in his arms and claimed her mouth with his.

He could tell he'd shocked her by the way her body momentarily went rigid against his. But her unyielding stiffness lasted only a mere heartbeat, then she seemed to melt against him.

Her arms, which had hung at her sides, came up

around his neck, and her lips opened beneath his, like a flower blossoming to the warmth of the sun.

Madness. It was utter madness, and the insanity apparently claimed them both. Talbot pulled her more firmly against him, wanting to feel the warmth, the sweet feminine curves of her body against his.

He felt the need to savor every sensation, to capture every nuance of the woman, the kiss and the intimacy of their bodies pressed so close. He knew all too quickly sanity would return and with it regret.

But regret seemed far away as he plundered the sweetness of her mouth, his hands roaming at will up and down the slender curve of her back.

Neither of them spoke, as if knowing a single word, a mere whisper, might shatter the magic of the moment. Her breasts were pressed against his chest, and he could feel her heartbeat crashing against his, a counter-rhythm of desire.

He wanted to sweep her up in his arms, carry her to his room and lose himself in her. He wanted to see her on his bed, her silky skin naked and her honey hair splayed against the blue of his bedspread.

A door slammed someplace in the distance. The front door. ''Mom?'' Andrew's voice called out.

Talbot released her and she stumbled back from him, her facial expression one of shell-shocked horror. She raised a trembling hand and touched her lips, then turned toward the kitchen door as Andrew and Richard entered.

"The movie stunk. We left after half an hour of suffering," Richard said. He looked from Talbot to Elizabeth. "Everything all right here?"

"Fine. Everything is just fine. We were just finishing the cleanup in here." Elizabeth's voice sounded higher-pitched than usual.

Richard turned his gaze again to Talbot. "And have you forgiven me for my stupid remark?" His eyes were the soft brown of contrition.

In a flash, all the love Talbot felt for his brother filled his chest. He nodded. "Of course," he said. "Emotions are running high. We've all said and done things tonight that were crazy and stupid, things that are best forgotten."

He knew Elizabeth got his point from the way her shoulders stiffened and emotion flashed in her eyes.

Regret filled him, and he wasn't sure it was a regret that he'd kissed her, or a regret that he'd dismissed the kiss so casually.

"I'm going to hit the sack now. I'm beat." He murmured a good-night, then left the kitchen and escaped to the privacy of his bedroom.

Once there, he closed his door, but instead of getting into bed, he stood at the window and stared outside into the darkness of the night.

He'd been a fool. Kissing Elizabeth had been the most foolish, thoughtless thing he'd ever done. The taste of her still lingered in his mouth, and her familiar, feminine scent clung to him.

He'd fantasized kissing her many times in the past, but the fantasy hadn't lived up to the reality. She'd been softer, sweeter, hotter than he'd ever imagined. A desire more intense than any he'd ever experienced had rocketed through him as they kissed.

And now, in the wake of that desire, came shame. Flashes of memories whizzed through his head, memories of Richard.

He would always feel the warmth of Richard holding tight to him as they ran away from the pond. "Save me, Talbot. Save me," Richard had screamed as they'd run from old man North and his gun.

"Don't worry, Richard. I'll never let anything bad happen to you," Talbot had promised.

He closed his eyes as he remembered the many nights Richard crawled into bed with him after being frightened by a storm or a nightmare.

And Talbot remembered the night he'd had to tell his brother that their parents were dead. Richard had wept like a baby in Talbot's arms, not only grieving the loss, but also fearing the future.

Talbot had assured his brother that everything would be okay and that he would take care of him. Talbot turned away from the window with a sigh of disgust.

And now Richard needed him more than ever. And Richard needed Elizabeth. And what was he, Talbot, doing? Lusting after Elizabeth.

As he undressed for bed, he thought of the flash of hurt that had darkened her eyes, the quick brace of her shoulders when he'd said that everyone had done or said something stupid tonight.

He knew his words had affected Elizabeth like a slap in the face. For he knew she'd been as caught up in the kiss, in the desire, as he had been.

It was better this way, he thought as he climbed into bed. Better that she be wary of him, keep her distance from him. He didn't want to have any more deep talks with her, didn't want to be in her head. He didn't want to share her thoughts or know her dreams. And he didn't want to share his own with her.

It was bad enough she'd nearly witnessed his emotional free fall while they'd been in his bedroom. It had frightened him, how close he'd been to losing it. And he absolutely had to remain strong— for Richard.

The devil in lipstick. He'd invited temptation into his home, and for a brief moment, he'd yielded to her temptation. But no more.

He was not about to sacrifice Richard's well-being for an irrational lust for Elizabeth.

Chapter Eight

"Everything all right?" Richard asked as Talbot left the room.

"Fine." Elizabeth flashed him a smile that felt false and forced. She wondered if her lips looked as bruised and swollen as they felt. She wondered if her face reflected the awesome desire she'd just experienced. "How would you two like some ice-cream cake? It was the reward for winning the pizza bake-off."

"Me! I want some!" Andrew exclaimed, seemingly oblivious to the tension that had momentarily filled the kitchen. He scooted into a chair at the table. "But I think you should have to say who the winner was."

"I think we all won," Richard said before Elizabeth could reply. "We had a good time making pizza and laughing together, and so that makes all of us winners."

"Your dad is right. Everyone's a winner." Elizabeth busied herself putting pieces of cake on plates, grateful for the activity to take her mind off the miasma of emotions that raged in her.

The kiss had rocked her to her very core, stoked an inferno of desire in her the likes of which she'd never known. Her heart still beat unnaturally fast, and her nerve endings felt electrified.

She sat at the table and sipped a cup of coffee while Richard and Andrew ate their cake and chattered about the inane things important to a nine-year-old boy. She tried to focus on the conversation, but couldn't.

She was filled with Talbot. Her mind, her senses, her heart was alive with him. Her breasts throbbed with the desire to be touched by his fingers, and her stomach ached with the pain of unfulfillment.

And in a single statement, he'd told her exactly what he'd felt about the kiss. It had been a stupid, crazy thing that had happened because emotions were running high.

And what had it been to her? Earth-shattering. Soul-searing. Like coming home after a long absence. And that scared her to death.

"Mom?" The tone of Andrew's voice indicated that he'd tried to get her attention more than once.

She focused on him, guilt tearing through her. "Dad asked you if you wanted to go bowling tomorrow afternoon." She could tell from her son's eager expression that he wanted her to join them.

"I'd love to go bowling," she said. She certainly didn't want to stay here with Talbot while Richard and Andrew were gone. She needed to keep as much distance as possible between Talbot and her.

And for the next five days, Talbot appeared to be working just as hard at avoiding being alone with her. In the morning, while Andrew worked with his tutor and Richard disappeared into town by himself, Elizabeth remained in her room or in the kitchen with Rose.

During the times she was alone, she found herself thinking about the conversation she and Talbot had had before that devastating kiss.

Had she contributed to Richard's immaturity by expecting nothing more from him? They say people rose to expectations. By expecting so little from him, had she and Talbot both somehow stymied Richard's growth?

She'd always believed herself to be fiercely independent, and she'd considered that a positive trait. But now she found herself wondering if perhaps she hadn't been a little selfish, as well. She'd never shared her fears, her burdens, her problems with Richard. She'd kept him out of the very private areas of herself because she knew no other way.

However, in those two days in the woods with Talbot, she'd shared more with him than she'd ever dreamed of sharing with Richard.

When Richard had questioned why she needed a night-light in the bedroom, she'd told him she liked to be able to see the way to the bathroom in the middle of the night. She'd never breathed a word about the trauma that had left her with a lifetime of fear of the dark. So why had she shared that with Talbot and not with the man who'd been her husband?

She didn't want to know the answer, feared what it might be. All she knew was that Talbot was right: they both had contributed to Richard's lack of maturity in at least a small way.

One other thing became clear to her. Talbot's kiss had confirmed that, although she'd cared about Richard, had desperately wanted to make a family with him, she'd never really loved him.

There had been little passion in their marriage. The kiss from Talbot had evoked more want in her than any lovemaking she and Richard had done.

And in avoiding Talbot for those five days, she found herself spending a lot of time with Andrew and Richard. They went bowling, to the movies and ate ice cream at the quaint little parlor in town.

She was surprised to find a new maturity in Richard. There was a new soberness in his eyes, and he appeared as if he'd turned a bit more inward and was seeking the man he could be.

She and Andrew had been in the McCarthy home a little more than a week when Richard got them up early for a sunrise horseback ride.

Elizabeth dressed in a pair of worn jeans and a hot-pink sweatshirt. She hurriedly pulled her hair up in a careless ponytail and went without makeup, aware that Richard and Andrew were eagerly awaiting her down by the corral.

Her heart leaped as she reached the corral and saw Talbot already mounted on a magnificent black stallion. He was in a pair of jeans and a black turtleneck sweater that emphasized the breadth of his shoulders.

Apparently Richard intended this as a complete family affair, she thought, trying to avoid looking at Talbot.

"Do you know how to ride?" Talbot asked, his voice the cool monotone he'd used when speaking to her ever since the kiss.

She grabbed the saddle horn of the mount Richard held for her and pulled herself up and into the saddle. "Foster family number five had horses," she explained. "I tried to ride every day for the six months I was there."

"And up you go," Richard said, helping Andrew into the saddle of the small horse the boy rode whenever he came to visit.

The morning sun was just peeking over the horizon, sending out brilliant pinks and oranges across the sky as they set off from the corral. The leaves on the trees were just beginning to change colors, donning splendid gold and rust tones.

They rode at a leisurely pace, the horses shaking their heads and snorting with eagerness in the brisk morning air.

"It's going to be a beautiful day," Talbot said, and he offered a quicksilver smile to Elizabeth.

The smile broke the ice, the tension Elizabeth felt had existed between them for the past week. "Yes, it is," she agreed, hoping they could get past that moment of insanity and return to the camaraderie and friendliness they'd enjoyed before the kiss.

"Won't be many more days warm enough for an early-morning ride," Richard observed. He smiled at Andrew. "This winter we'll build the biggest snowman in the world."

Hope. Somewhere in the past week, Richard had found hope for the future. Elizabeth's heart expanded. She knew it was vital for Richard to maintain a positive attitude in the battle ahead. She hoped he and Andrew had lots of winters together.

It was easy to feel positive as the four of them rode across the green pastures in the sweet-scented air. Elizabeth rode just behind the three men, her gaze lingering on Talbot.

He looked more relaxed, more at ease than she'd

seen him in the past week. He was a natural in the saddle, sitting tall and easily commanding the powerful horse beneath him with a mere flick of the reins.

As always, just looking at him evoked myriad emotions. She could no longer deny that she was overwhelmingly drawn to him on a physical level. He stirred her in a way no other man had ever done. And, as much as she hated to admit it, something about him touched her heart.

They rode for about thirty minutes, and when they reached the peak of a hill, Richard said he wanted to talk to them and asked that they all dismount.

They got off their horses and stood in a circle, their attention focused on Richard. "I just wanted to thank you all for this time we've had together," he began. "You'll never know how much this has meant to me."

Talbot frowned, obviously ill at ease about his brother's heartfelt thanks. "Richard..."

Richard held up a hand. "Let me finish," he said firmly. "I know I haven't been the best brother, husband or father." He wrapped an arm around Andrew's neck and pulled the boy close against him. "But I want you to know that you are the most important people in my life, and I'll never be able to repay you for being here for me."

"You don't have to repay us," Elizabeth said,

emotion rising to tighten her chest. "We love you, Richard."

"I know. And that's why I've scheduled the surgery for first thing Monday morning. The surgery will be done in Kansas City. The doctor didn't want me to wait any longer, and I want to get well—I need to get well so I can prove to you all that I'm worth the effort."

"You don't have to prove anything to anyone," Talbot said, his voice deeper than usual.

"Dad, I think you're the best in the world," Andrew put in. Elizabeth's heart nearly exploded as father and son embraced.

Please God, she pleaded silently. Please let Richard come through the surgery with flying colors. Don't make my son live the rest of his life without a father. Don't take Richard from us.

"Hey, Dad," Andrew said as Richard released him. "I hate to be a pain, but I've got to go to the bathroom."

"I'll take him back," Elizabeth said.

"No, you wait here. I'll take him back to the house," Richard insisted as he and Andrew remounted. "We'll be back in a little while."

Before Elizabeth could formulate a reasonable protest, Richard and Andrew rode off, leaving her alone with Talbot.

It was ridiculous how her heart instantly began banging a new rhythm. Ridiculous and irritating.

"So it sounds like we'll be out of your hair as of Monday," she finally said to break the tense silence that had sprung up between them. "If Richard is having the surgery in Kansas City, then Andrew and I will go back home."

"I haven't minded having you and Andrew in the house," he replied, his eyes dark and glittering. "The ten days you've been here, the house hasn't seemed quite so big, not quite as..." He frowned. "Not quite as empty."

For just a moment, she'd thought he was going to say lonely. But that was crazy. Strong, independent men like Talbot didn't get lonely. Just like strong, independent women like her didn't get lonely.

But she *was* lonely, and scared, and aching with the need to be held by somebody as strong and independent and lonely as her.

From the moment Richard had told her about his brain tumor, Elizabeth had remained strong. She'd been strong for Richard, strong for her son, displaying optimism and hope and refusing to face the fear that hid in the shadows of her heart. But now Richard's surgery was to take place in two days, and her fear stepped out of the shadows and into the harsh light of the morning sun.

"Talbot?" Her voice was shaky, and to her horror, the vision of him blurred as her eyes filled with unexpected tears. She said nothing more, but merely took a step forward, her arms reaching out to him.

Talbot saw her disintegrating before his very eyes. Her eyes, those sky-blue eyes, filled with tears that trekked down her cheeks, and her lower lip trembled with despair.

He knew that to touch her, reach out to her was wrong, but he couldn't help himself. He felt her need for him, and he couldn't deny his own need for her.

He gathered her into his arms and breathed in the sweet scent of her hair as he fought the emotion that tore through his chest.

Whatever control she'd had broke as she clung to him, deep, silent sobs shaking her body against his. He held her tightly, felt her grief, her fear, and wished he could take it from her so she wouldn't have to suffer. Her tears broke his heart—a heart that was already half-broken by his brother's plight.

"Shh," he whispered against her ear, his hands rubbing her slender back in an attempt to soothe. She didn't make a sound, although her emotions dampened the front of his shirt and racked her body with tremors.

"I'm sorry," she said through her tears, as if embarrassed by her display. "I'm so sorry." She tried to pull away, but he held her fast.

"Don't be sorry," he said. "Let it go. Let it all out."

Once again she leaned into him, as if not possessing the strength to step away. Within minutes, her sobbing had stopped, but still she remained in his embrace.

He stroked a hand down her hair, felt the warmth of the sun residing in the silky strands. "Better?" he asked softly.

She nodded. "I'm so scared," she said after a moment had passed. She looked up at him, those blue eyes of hers seeming to see deep inside him. "Are you scared, Talbot?"

He hesitated. He had never confessed fear to anyone. Not even Rose, who knew him better than anyone, knew of the fear he'd suffered first as a young man responsible for the much younger Richard, and now, when faced with his brother's illness.

"Yes, I'm scared," he confessed. "To tell the truth, I'm terrified."

She placed her palms on either side of his face. "And when you're scared, who holds you? When the darkness is everywhere around you, who makes you feel safe? Who makes you feel as if eventually the darkness will lift?"

"Nobody. I've never needed anyone. Until now." He dipped his head and touched his lips to hers. It was the softest of kisses, a mere whisper of a touch.

She moaned. It was not the moan of a woman

gathering her emotions, nor was it the sound of a woman in anguish. It came from the very depths of her, and it was a moan of desire.

The kiss Talbot had meant to keep light and uncomplicated suddenly became a kiss of searing want. Her hands circled his neck as his tongue touched her lower lip, seeking entry.

And she allowed him in, opening her mouth to him as her body molded to his. Reason faded as Talbot responded to her smell, her taste, and gave himself over to the sensual volcano that holding her evoked in him.

As the kiss deepened, he ran his hands up beneath her sweatshirt, wanting, needing to touch her silky skin. And it was silky, and warm and smooth. The skin on her back beckoned him to explore further.

Their breathing became more rapid, he could feel the racing of her heart, matching the speed of his. The intensity nearly stole his breath away.

His hands moved from her back to her sides, where he felt her rib cage beneath his fingertips. Up they swept, until they encountered the elastic band of her bra.

She gasped as his hands moved over her breasts. And through the lace and silk of her bra, he could feel the pebble hardness as her nipples rose in response.

Out of control. Someplace in the back of his mind, he knew he was out of control. For the first time in his life, he wasn't considering consequences or thinking about tomorrow. He was thinking only of this moment and this woman. Elizabeth. Sweet Elizabeth. Strong Elizabeth.

He wanted to lay her down in the sweet-smelling grass, take her clothes off slowly and reveal the charms of her body. He wanted to make love to her, possess her as no other man ever had.

The thought sent ice through his veins. The icy waters of reality. Disgust roared through him—disgust for his desire, disgust for himself.

He dropped his hands, broke the kiss and stepped back from her. She looked as beautiful as he'd ever seen her, with her lips reddened from his kisses, her hair tousled by his fingers and the wind, and her eyes deepened by a hazy fog of desire.

He drew a breath and raked a hand through his hair. "It's obvious there's some sort of chemistry at work between us," he said, irritated that his voice sounded slightly unsteady. "I'm not going to lie, Elizabeth. I want you. I want you in my arms…in my bed. I have never in my life wanted a woman as much as I want you."

Her eyes flared at his words, but she said nothing.

"Don't mistake what I'm saying. I want you, but it's strictly a physical want. And I am not about to jeopardize my relationship with my brother or his mental well-being for a brief fling with you."

He saw the hurt that his words inflicted, but he

had to make certain this didn't happen again. He knew if he found her in his arms one more time, he wouldn't be able to stop before a dreadful mistake was made.

"It's pure lust, Elizabeth, and I don't trust myself when I'm around you," he said as he remounted his horse. "After Richard's surgery, I think it's best if we don't see each other again."

He didn't wait for her reply, but instead, took off at a gallop and didn't look back.

He rode hard and fast, with the cool autumn air slapping him in the face, trying to outrun the desire that still heated his blood, that still coursed through his veins.

Elizabeth. Her name was a curse on his lips, in his heart, as he pushed the horse faster and faster. Two more days, he told himself. He would only have to be around her for two more days, then they would never have to see each other again.

It was nearly noon when Talbot finally returned to the house. He took a quick shower, dressed, then headed out for the offices in Topeka.

He could lose himself in work, had done it a hundred times in the past. As long as he had McCarthy Industries, the legacy from his father, he didn't need anything or anyone else.

He worked through dinner, grabbing a sandwich from a vending machine and eating at his desk. He continued to work into the evening hours, reluctant to go home.

Darkness had long fallen when he finally left the building and got into his car to head back to Morning View. Instantly, the dark reminded him of Elizabeth.

He thought of her as a five-year-old, torn away from everything she had ever known, without the comfort of family. He wished he could have been there for her. He wished he'd known her when she'd been five, wished he'd known her all her life.

Turning on the radio, he filled the interior of the car with raucous rock and roll, hoping to make thought impossible. He kept the radio blaring until he pulled into the driveway of his home.

There was only one light burning in the house—the light in the living room. The rest of the house was dark, and he hoped everyone was asleep. He didn't want to see anyone or talk to anyone.

Quietly, he let himself in the front door and instantly heard the soft murmur of voices coming from the living room. He recognized the voices. Elizabeth and Richard.

He peered into the living room and his heart seemed to stop. They stood together in front of the window, their arms wrapped around each other in an embrace. He couldn't hear the words they spoke to each other; in truth, he didn't want to hear.

As Talbot watched his brother stroke her tawny hair, a horrible knowledge exploded in Talbot's chest.

Talbot realized he was in love with Elizabeth.

Chapter Nine

"**P**romise me," Richard said to Elizabeth as he broke the embrace.

Elizabeth had been on her way to bed when she'd seen Richard sitting alone in the living room. She'd come in to see if he was all right. He'd apparently just needed to talk. They'd talked briefly about their marriage, spoken in depth about Andrew and touched on the surgery.

"What?" She stepped away from him.

His brown eyes peered intently into hers. "Promise me we'll always be friends. It's important to me, and I think it's important to Andrew."

"That's a promise that's easy to keep," she assured him.

"Even if one or both of us remarry, we'll still be

friends.'' Elizabeth nodded and he continued. ''And promise me one other thing. If something happens during the surgery, tell Andrew I was a great guy. Tell him I was brave and strong and that I loved him more than anything on earth.''

Tears burned at Elizabeth's eyes. She dashed them away. ''Nothing is going to happen during the surgery except that the doctor is going to get that tumor out of your head,'' she said firmly. ''Besides, I don't have to tell Andrew those things. He already knows them.''

Richard flashed her a bright smile. ''Thanks, Elizabeth.''

She nodded. ''And now I'd better get upstairs and tuck Andrew in. He never goes to sleep until I kiss him good-night.''

Elizabeth found her son just the way she'd expected to find him. In bed, but not asleep. He sat up as she entered the room. ''I thought maybe you forgot about me.''

She smiled and sat on the edge of his bed. ''Not a chance. You doing okay?'' She smoothed a strand of hair away from his forehead.

''Sure.''

''Are you going to be all right here tomorrow when we leave for Kansas City?'' Elizabeth and Richard had agreed that the best plan of action was for Andrew to remain here in Morning View with Rose until after the surgery was finished and Richard was in recovery. The morning after the surgery, Elizabeth would drive back here to retrieve her son.

"Yeah. Rose is gonna teach me how to cook some good stuff. I want to learn how to bake a cake for when Dad gets better."

"That would be nice." Elizabeth leaned down and kissed her son's cheek.

"And you'll call me from the hospital as soon as Dad is out of surgery?"

"I promise," she replied.

His big brown eyes gazed at her soberly. "Will you promise me that he's going to be all right?"

Elizabeth's heart ached at her son's question. She desperately wished she could make this promise to him, but she knew better. She remembered what she'd told Talbot and now repeated the words to her son.

"Honey, there are some things you can't promise. I'm not the one in control of this. Do you understand?"

He nodded. "I said a prayer for Dad."

"That's all we can do," Elizabeth replied. Once again she leaned forward and kissed his forehead. "Now, you get a good night's sleep."

As she left her son's bedroom, tears once again burned in her eyes. She'd been on the verge of an emotional meltdown all day long, ever since that moment Talbot had jumped on his horse and ridden away from her.

She went into her bedroom and closed the door, fighting the wave of emotion that threatened to consume her.

Between the trauma of Richard's imminent surgery and the shock and confusion of those moments with Talbot in the early-morning sun, she felt ridiculously fragile and overwhelmed at a time when she needed her strength most.

Richard and his needs were now pretty much out of her hands. Tomorrow they would check him into the hospital, and first thing the next morning he would go into surgery. There was nothing more she could do to help him prepare for what was ahead.

And there was nothing she could do to help Talbot. As she undressed and pulled on her cotton nightgown, her body burned with the memory of his touch, the fire in his kiss.

"I have never in my life wanted a woman as much as I want you." His words haunted her, fired a flame inside her she feared would never be doused. She crawled into bed, aided by the glow of the night-light he'd bought her.

And she had never in her life wanted a man as much as she wanted Talbot. Had he wished, he could have taken her right there in the grass, with the morning sun beating down on them. She would have eagerly succumbed to the heat of his hands and the magic of his kiss.

Even though he'd told her it was nothing but lust,

she still wanted him. She wanted him because she loved him.

She sat straight up, her heart pounding with the realization. She loved Talbot. She loved him with all her heart and all her soul.

She had no idea when the love had first occurred, how long she'd hidden the truth of her feelings for him from herself. But there was no hiding now. Her love for him was an ache inside her, a torment for which there was no relief.

He'd said he wanted her, lusted for her, but he hadn't mentioned love. And even if he had, what would be the point?

Even though she knew without a doubt that she and Richard would share no future together other than in the raising of their son, how would Richard react if his ex-wife became involved with his brother?

Tomorrow they would take Richard to the hospital, and the next day he would have his surgery. And after that she and Talbot would have no reason to ever see each other again.

It was best that way. Best that she forget the gentle heat of his touch, the fiery flames of his kiss.

She turned onto her side and squeezed her eyes tightly closed, blocking out the glow of the nightlight and trying desperately to block out the glow of the newly recognized love in her heart.

At noon the next day, they set off on the drive to

Kansas City. Elizabeth insisted on following the two men in her own car, preferring her isolation and knowing she'd need to drive herself back to Morning View after the surgery to collect Andrew.

She followed them directly to the hospital, where it took only a few minutes to get Richard checked into a room. After seeing that he was settled and comfortable, Elizabeth left, promising to return early the next morning.

She felt no sense of homecoming or welcome when she walked into her apartment. The place felt cold, empty and achingly lonely.

The evening hours crept by. She called Andrew and talked with him until he got bored, then called Richard and spoke with him. They talked of the future, about Andrew growing and Richard being there to share in his adult years.

She was pleased to hear the ring of optimism in Richard's voice and was grateful he seemed to be approaching the surgery in good spirits.

A prayer for Richard's well-being was on her lips as she got into bed that night. As she waited for sleep to claim her, she wondered where Talbot was spending the night.

If things had been different between them, had their relationship been a normal one of ex-brother and sister-in-law, she might have offered him the use of Andrew's room for the night.

But with the situation between them as volatile as

it was, the last thing she could do was actively seek time alone with him. It was bad enough she would be spending the hours of the surgery with him.

She desperately wished she could go to sleep tonight loving him and awake the next morning with all love gone from her heart. No lingering effects, no residual pain, just a quick and easy sleep fix against the addiction of love.

A rueful smile curved her lips. If she could figure out a cure for love, she'd be the heroine of unhappy lovers everywhere and wealthy beyond her wildest imaginings.

Instead, she had to figure out how to forget Talbot. And best to forget that the man she'd fallen in love with was the one man she would never, ever have.

Talbot had never known the minutes in an hour could move so slowly. He paced the small confines of the waiting room, trying desperately to ignore Elizabeth, who was the only other occupant at the moment.

He looked at his watch and sighed. Richard had been in surgery less than two hours. And the doctor had told them the surgery would last from five to six hours. It was going to be one hell of a long day.

"I'm going down to the cafeteria for a cup of coffee," he said. "You want to come?"

He half hoped she said no. They had not spoken

more than two words to each other since they'd arrived at the hospital just after six that morning. They'd sat in Richard's room until he'd been wheeled away, then they'd moved to the waiting room.

She stood. "Yes, I'd love a cup of coffee." Her gaze didn't quite meet his.

Together they left the waiting room and headed for the elevator that would take them to the cafeteria in the basement.

Talbot steeled himself against her invasion of his senses as they stood in the small enclosure of the elevator. The sweet scent of her seemed to call to him, but he fought the temptation she represented. She looked beautiful, cheerful and bright in a royal-blue dress that did amazing things to her eyes.

He frowned. Seeing her and Richard standing together in an embrace the night before had reminded him just how important it was that he stay away from her. Richard obviously needed her. It didn't matter if Richard wanted a second chance at their marriage. He needed her in his life, and Talbot couldn't, wouldn't interfere.

They reached the cafeteria, where she got a cup of coffee and a bagel, and he got coffee and a muffin. They found a table and sat across from each other.

He took a sip of his coffee and eyed her thoughtfully.

Yes, she was beautiful, but he couldn't help but notice the faint shadows beneath her eyes.

"You look tired," he said.

She smiled wearily. "I am tired. I'm tired in my body and tired in my mind." She sighed and tore off a tiny piece of bagel. "To say these last few days have been stressful is an understatement. But you must be tired, too."

"I am," he said grudgingly. He didn't want to feel the same things she did, didn't want the intimacy of experiencing the same emotions. He was not only tired in his body and mind, he was weary in his soul.

He hadn't realized before now that he believed in true love, in soul mates. He hadn't realized the flicker of hope that had always been with him—the hope that eventually he would find his one true love and live happily ever after.

The knowledge that he'd found that love with the one woman he couldn't have hurt more than he'd ever thought possible. He felt as if he'd lost something—before he'd ever really found it.

"Richard seemed to be in wonderful spirits this morning," she said, pulling him from his thoughts.

He nodded. "We had a long talk last night, and once this surgery is behind him, apparently he intends to make some big changes."

"Changes?" She frowned. "What kind of changes?"

"First of all, he no longer intends to work for McCarthy Industries." She looked as shocked as Talbot had felt the night before when Richard had told him how much he hated what he did for a living.

"Really? What does he want to do?"

Talbot paused and took a sip of the strong coffee. "He isn't sure. He wants to go to college, see what options are available." He hesitated a moment, unsure if he wanted to confess what else Richard had told him.

"I'm shocked," she exclaimed. "He's worked for you since we got married. He never breathed a word about being unhappy."

Talbot sighed. "I think he's been unhappy for a very long time. He told me last night that he's always hated working for me. He figures the only reason he was hired was because he was a McCarthy. He also wants to get his own apartment, is tired of living with me and not having to be responsible for himself. I've carried him for too long, made life too easy for him."

Elizabeth stared at him. "And now you're carrying a wealth of guilt thinking that maybe Richard's immaturity has been your fault all along."

Talbot didn't reply, although she'd nailed his feelings square on the head. To his immense surprise, she laughed. "I certainly don't know what you find amusing,'' he said, forcing all the coolness he could into his voice and his expression.

She further surprised him by laughing once again. ''You used to be able to intimidate me with that cold, arrogant tone and expression, but you can't anymore. And I find it amusing that I struggled with the same issues last night after going to bed. Worrying that it was all my fault that Richard hadn't grown up while we were married. We're far too much alike, Talbot. We want to take all the credit when things are good, and want all the blame when things are bad. You become selfish when you're used to being alone for so long.''

He straightened, wanting to deny that he was selfish, wanting to deny that they were anything alike. She held up a hand to stop whatever he wanted to say.

''Stop beating yourself up, Talbot. You're a good man, and you did the best you could, just as I did. It's time to let go and allow Richard the freedom to make his own way in life, the freedom to succeed or fail.''

She said all the words he'd told himself but had needed to hear from another. Again he was struck by the knowledge that had the situation been different, they might have melded and become one heart.

He stood abruptly, afraid to spend any more time with her, afraid if he did, he might speak of the love that burned in his heart. And by verbalizing his feelings for her, he feared he'd give a piece of himself away—a piece he would never be able to retrieve.

He would ruin things with his brother, who needed all the love and support Talbot could offer.

"I need to go for a walk," he said. Without waiting for her to reply, he strode away.

Elizabeth watched him go, wondering why it seemed that lately she was always left staring at his back.

She took a sip of her coffee, their brief conversation replaying in her mind. What she'd wanted to say to him was that it was impossible to be intimidated by a man who had held her through the long hours of a dark night. It was impossible to feel intimidated by a man who had remembered her fear and bought her a night-light. Finally, it was impossible to be intimidated by the man she loved.

And she'd come perilously close to telling him she loved him. The words had burned on the tip of her tongue, crying to be released.

She finished her bagel and coffee, then returned to the waiting room. Talbot wasn't there, and her thoughts shifted from him to his brother. Checking her watch, she realized only three hours had passed. Another two to wait, to worry, and to pray.

During the next two hours, people drifted in and out of the waiting room. Family members hovered together, holding hands and murmuring softly as they awaited a loved one's prognosis. Talbot returned to the room and paced restlessly, his forehead creased with lines of worry.

Elizabeth watched him, aching as she saw how isolated he appeared. Or was it her own isolation that pierced deeply into her heart?

She'd always believed herself strong enough to be alone for the rest of her life, if necessary. But she no longer felt strong. She was alone and wished she had warm male arms to hold her. Talbot's arms. Loving Talbot had woken a need in her, a need she'd never before realized she'd possessed.

When the five hours had passed and still the doctor hadn't appeared to tell them how the surgery had gone, Elizabeth left the waiting room and went to sit in the small chapel.

There were only five pews and a small altar with candles burning, but she instantly felt a modicum of peace as she sank into the first pew.

She stared at the flickering candlelight, not consciously schooling her thoughts in any particular direction, but rather allowing them to roam free.

She knew how much she and Talbot were alike. Both strong and independent, both self-sufficient through necessity and life's hard knocks, but she wondered if he felt the same core of emptiness that she did.

Lust, she reminded herself. That was what he'd said he felt for her. And lust had nothing to do with sharing dreams, holding tightly to each other through good times and bad. Lust had nothing to do with love.

Consciously, she willed him out of her mind and again focused on Richard. He had to be all right. He just had to be, she thought fervently. She couldn't imagine having to tell her son that his father had passed away. She couldn't imagine telling Andrew that he would have to live the rest of his life without the father he so dearly loved.

She smelled Talbot's familiar scent a mere second before he sat down on the pew next to her. She stiffened, needing every defense against him.

"No word yet," he said, and sighed. The sound of that sigh, so weary, so deep, tugged at her. Despite her resolve to the contrary, she found his hand and laced her fingers with his.

He tensed, then his fingers gently squeezed hers. "I'm can't imagine my life without him in it," he said softly. "He makes me laugh, and he makes me want to kick him in the rear, but I can't imagine him not being here."

She said nothing, knew there were no words that could soothe him. She simply returned his squeeze and hoped he understood that she felt the same.

She had no idea how long they sat there, not speaking, merely holding hands and staring at the candles, silent prayers filling their hearts.

Dr. Breshnahan found them there. Still in his

scrubs, a weariness etching deep lines into his face, he greeted them with a triumphant smile. "It went well," he said as Talbot and Elizabeth stood. "It looks like we got all of the tumor. We'll schedule him for some chemo just to be on the safe side."

"Thank God!" Talbot exclaimed, his eyes overbright.

"Can we see him?" Elizabeth asked.

"He's in the recovery room now and just coming around. I'll have a nurse come and get you in about fifteen minutes, and you can go in to see him for a brief visit."

As the doctor left them alone once again, a swell of emotion filled Elizabeth. Suddenly she was in Talbot's arms, pulled against him as he released a laugh of sheer joy. "Richard is going to be all right," he said.

"He's going to live a long life," she replied, gazing up at the man she loved with all her heart. "He's going to continue to make us crazy, and he'll be around to see Andrew grow into a man and build a family of his own."

She burst into tears.

"Hey, hey," he protested. "What's with the tears? It's not the time to cry. It's time to celebrate."

"I know...I know." She stepped out of his embrace, needing to put distance between them. "I'm happy. I'm so happy Richard is going to be all

right.'' She swiped angrily at the tears that continued to fall, unable to control their descent.

"Then why are you crying?'' His voice was soft,
tender, and it was her complete undoing.

She drew a deep breath, unable to keep her gaze
on him. She stared at the burning candles, their flickering flames now blurs. "I'm crying because I know
it's time for me to tell you goodbye.'' The words
fell from her lips, words she could no longer hold
back, emotions she could no longer suppress.

She finally looked at him. "I'm crying because I
love you, Talbot. And I'm crying because I don't
know how I'm going to live without you.''

At that moment a nurse stepped into the chapel.
"Dr. Breshnahan says I can take you to Richard
now.''

"Thank you,'' Talbot said. He pulled a handker-
chief from his pocket and held it out to Elizabeth.
"Here. Don't let Richard see your tears.'' Without
looking at her, he followed the nurse from the tiny
chapel where Elizabeth's words of love echoed in
the resounding emptiness.

Chapter Ten

Elizabeth hurriedly dabbed at her eyes and followed, appalled by the confession that had just left her lips. How could she have lost all control? How could she have blurted out her innermost feelings?

And he'd said not a word in reply. It had been as if she'd been speaking of the weather, or a shopping experience, something mundane and boring, something that had absolutely nothing to do with him. His face had remained a mask of granite, without expression.

Embarrassment burned in her cheeks. What had she been thinking? What on earth had she hoped to gain? Dear God, she hadn't been thinking. She'd been beyond thought, functioning only on sheer emotion.

And now she once again had to reach inside and retrieve the strength that had always seen her through, the strength that had helped her through a childhood of isolation, a marriage of disappointment and so many years of empty loneliness.

When she entered the semidark recovery room, Talbot already stood at Richard's side. She moved to the other side of Richard, carefully keeping her gaze off Talbot.

"Hi," she said to Richard. He looked half-asleep, obviously still fighting the last of the anesthesia, but he offered her a groggy smile. His head was bandaged and he was hooked to a variety of machines that dripped and beeped and clicked and pulsed.

"Did Talbot tell you? They got it all. You're going to be fine, just fine," she assured him.

Talbot touched his brother's shoulder. "All you need to do right now is rest."

Richard tried to sit up, his mouth working to form words. "You have to...you have to call..."

"I know," Elizabeth said. "I'll call Andrew right away and tell him you're fine." She patted his shoulder in an effort to get him to lie back and relax, but he remained agitated.

"And...you have to call...call Erica."

Elizabeth's gaze shot to Talbot. He stared at his brother. "Richard, who the hell is Erica?" he asked.

The smile that curved Richard's mouth was the most loving, the most beautiful Elizabeth had ever seen. "She's...she's the woman I'm going to marry."

With this startling announcement, Richard relaxed and fell back asleep. Elizabeth looked up and met Talbot's gaze. "It's obviously the effects of the anesthesia," he said. "He's dreaming or delusional. Or maybe he meant to say your name, but he's all confused."

She nodded absently and sat in the chair next to Richard's bed. She wasn't sure what to believe. Erica? She'd never heard Richard mention her before.

Was it possible Richard had been dating somebody? Had he found somebody he had fallen in love with?

She waited for a reaction in her heart, but there was none. If Richard had found love, then she was happy for him. She hoped he'd have a long and glorious marriage.

But if he'd been seeing somebody, wouldn't Talbot have known? Talbot always seemed to know everything about his brother's life. No, Talbot was probably right. Richard's words were the aftereffects of the anesthesia.

Richard slept for only about ten minutes—ten minutes with Talbot on one side and Elizabeth on the other.

They spoke not a word, and Elizabeth didn't look at him as they waited.

Her humiliation was complete where he was concerned. She'd bared her heart, and he'd handed her a hankie to dry her tears. She couldn't look at him. She was afraid she'd see scorn or pity in his eyes.

Later, when she was all alone, she would grieve for what would never be. At the moment she would focus on Richard.

This time when he opened his eyes, he seemed more alert. He struggled to sit up a bit, then smiled at his brother. "I'm tougher than you thought, right?"

Talbot smiled. "I always knew you were tough."

"I came through with flying colors, right?"

"Right," Talbot agreed. "We McCarthys are a tough bunch."

Richard smiled, then turned and looked at Elizabeth. "I need you to do me a favor," he said.

"Call Erica?"

He looked at her in surprise. "I already asked you to?"

She nodded. "But I can't call her until you give me a number or at least a last name."

"And who is Erica?" Talbot asked again.

Again a soft smile curved Richard's lips. "Erica Taylor. She moved to Morning View about six months ago, and we've been dating ever since. I didn't tell her about the tumor...about the surgery. I...I didn't want to worry her."

He didn't want to worry Erica. Elizabeth saw a light in Richard's eyes that she'd never seen before.

"Taylor?" Talbot asked. "Is she related to Zelda Taylor?"

"Erica is Zelda's granddaughter. She moved to Morning View to care for Zelda. Since Zelda passed away, Erica's been having a hard time. She doesn't really know anyone in Morning View except me. She...she needs me."

Elizabeth saw the love that shone on Richard's face. Erica needed him, and Richard apparently needed to be needed—something Elizabeth had never given him. "If you write down her number for me, I'll go give her a call," Elizabeth said as she pulled a slip of paper from her purse.

A few minutes later, after calling Andrew to let him know his father was doing fine, Elizabeth phoned the woman Richard intended to marry.

It took only a few minutes for Elizabeth to get the impression of a sweet, young woman who seemed to be utterly head over heels in love with Richard.

When Elizabeth hung up, she felt a sudden pang in her heart—a pang of bittersweetness as she realized Richard was moving on, building a life of his own that did not include her.

And she had to move on with her life, too—alone, without Talbot, without the man she loved. She steadied herself and returned to Richard's room, surprised to find him alone.

"What happened to your brother?" she asked as she slid back into the chair next to the hospital bed.

"He left. He told me he'd be back first thing in the morning."

He probably couldn't stand being in the same room with her, she thought. Especially after she'd been so stupid and told him she loved him.

"So you talked to Erica?" Richard asked.

She nodded. "She's on her way here. I wouldn't be surprised if she broke a couple of speed limits on the way. She was appalled that you didn't tell her about your condition."

"Will you sit with me until she gets here?" he asked.

Elizabeth hesitated only a moment, then nodded. "Of course." After all, what did she have to go home to? A silent apartment? A broken heart?

It was after seven by the time Erica Taylor arrived at the hospital. A petite, dark-haired woman, she rushed to Richard's side and burst into tears.

Elizabeth watched as Richard consoled her, showing a tenderness, a caring she'd never seen from him in all the years they'd been married.

Silently, Elizabeth backed out of the room, leaving the two of them alone.

It wasn't until she was in her car that all her emotions came crashing in on her. The hours of worry, the days of tense anxiety concerning Talbot, her humiliating confession to him and the memory of his face, so blank, so untouched by her words of love.

Overwhelmed, Elizabeth leaned her head against the steering wheel and cried. Her tears came from her very depths, all the tears stored for the sum of her lifetime.

She cried for the little girl who'd lost her parents, for the young woman who'd wanted so desperately not to be alone that she'd gotten pregnant and married a man who'd been too immature to fulfill her expectations.

Finally, she wept for the woman she'd become, a woman who'd always believed herself strong, but who'd finally identified her weakness: she loved a man she couldn't have, a man who wanted her, but didn't love her.

When her tears were finished falling, she felt emptier than she'd ever felt. Her heartbeat was nothing more than a dull echo of what had once been a vibrant muscle. Her stomach ached with the bereavement of love found, then lost.

She had never felt so alone.

At some point in the afternoon heavy clouds had filled the sky, and now night had fallen. The darkness was complete, unbroken by even a sliver of moonlight.

She had forgotten to turn on any lights when she'd left the place that morning. The apartment would be dark and empty. She didn't want to go inside.

But she couldn't have what she wanted.

Talbot.

His name sang through her. It was a sad song, to which if she listened for too long, would only make her cry again.

She got out of her car and straightened her shoulders. Time to get on with living. It wasn't as if she had nothing in her life. She had a beautiful son who would always bring her joy. She would go back to school and finish up her degree and eventually get a full-time job teaching young children.

She didn't need a man to fulfill her.

It took her only a moment to unlock her apartment door and open it. For a moment, she stood in the threshold, trying to make sense of the scene before her.

Candles.

They filled every surface of the room. Big ones, fat ones, tall ones, red, white, silver and gold ones. Their flames lit the room with a brilliant glow.

"I've been waiting for you."

She jumped at the sound of the deep, familiar voice and realized Talbot sat on one end of the sofa. She stepped inside and closed the door behind her, her mind still reeling. "Wh-what are you doing here?"

He stood, casting a tall, dark shadow on the wall

behind him. "What does it look like I'm doing here?" He gestured around. "I'm filling your darkness with light."

"I don't understand..." She was suddenly afraid—afraid this might be a terrible joke, afraid to trust the hope that filled her heart.

He walked to where she stood, stopping only when he was so close to her she could feel his breath on her face, smell the wonderful scent that was intrinsically his. "I want to be the candle you cling to each night. I want to be the light that makes you feel safe and secure. I want to illuminate every single space in your heart with my love for you."

"Your love?" She refused to yield to the need to throw herself into his arms—not until she was absolutely certain of what he was saying, what he was offering her. "But I thought...you told me it was just lust."

His eyes glittered in the candlelight, and the smile that curved his lips shot a spark of heat through her. "Oh, trust me. I lust for you, Elizabeth. I can't remember a time I didn't lust for you." He reached out and gently touched her cheek. "But it's more than lust, deeper than desire. I love you, Elizabeth. I love you with all my heart."

His words broke the inertia that had momentarily gripped her. She flew into his arms and lifted her face for his kiss. His mouth claimed hers in a kiss so sweet, so complete, it stole her breath.

His arms enfolded her close, and she felt as if she'd come home after a long, unwanted absence. The heart that had beat so listlessly only moments before now thundered with life.

When the kiss finally ended, he continued to hold her tightly against him. She wondered if she was living a dream.

"The most difficult thing I've ever done in my life was hearing you tell me this afternoon that you love me and trying to close my heart against your words. I couldn't allow your love in, not without knowing what Richard needed from you."

"My friendship. That's all he needs."

"I realize that now." Again his mouth possessed hers, as his hands on her back pressed her intimately close to him.

She reveled in his kiss, a kiss that did, indeed, seem to seek out each and every dark corner of her heart and fill them with brilliant warmth and light.

When this kiss ended, he took her by the hand and led her to the sofa. "If Richard hadn't told us about Erica, I would never have spoken of loving you," he said as they sat side by side, her hands clasped in his. "I would have never risked his mental well-being by opening my heart to you."

"I know that." And she only loved him more for it, that he was willing to sacrifice his own happiness for the sake of his brother's.

"I think I fell in love with you the first time I saw you," he said.

She looked at him in surprise. She'd never had a clue. "I always believed you didn't like me."

He shook his head and smiled ruefully. "I wanted to dislike you. But I took one look at you, glaring at me with those bold eyes, that chin tilted upward as if defying me to ruin your wedding plans, and I knew in another lifetime, in another world, I would have loved you."

"I don't know when I fell in love with you," she said truthfully. "But I know you always made me nervous, because I found you far too attractive." She smiled. "I used to feel like a participant on one of those tacky talk shows. You know, the ones with subjects like 'I'm in Love with My Husband's Brother.'"

"So marry me. We can appear on a tacky talk show with the subject 'I Married My Husband's Brother.'"

She laughed, then sobered. "Talbot, I love you with all my heart, and there is nothing I'd like better than to be your wife…"

"But?"

"But shouldn't we talk to Richard about all this?" She frowned thoughtfully. "You and Richard share a wonderful relationship. I don't want to come between you."

"Richard already knows. He and I talked when

you went to call Erica. He told me I'd be a fool to let you get away. We thought we were hiding our feelings for each other so well, but according to Richard, a blind man would have been able to see how we felt. He gave me his blessing. But before you agree to marry me, I want to make something perfectly clear.''

''What?'' The candlelight made his features appear sterner and more forbidding than ever, but his eyes shone with a softness, a sweet tenderness.

''I will be a more difficult husband than Richard ever was. I intend to share my days and nights with you. I'll want to know all about your dreams, commiserate with you about all your disappointments.'' He released one of her hands and stroked the side of her face. ''I love the fact that you're a strong woman, but I never want you to use that strength to close off from me. I want it all, Elizabeth. I don't just want your good, I want your bad, your fears, your sorrows. I want to be there for you so you'll never feel alone again.''

The flickering candles blurred into golden blobs as tears sprang to Elizabeth's eyes. ''Only on one condition,'' she said softly. ''I get all of you, as well.'' She reached up and placed her palms on either side of his beautiful face. ''I want your dreams and your hopes, and I want your fears and your sorrows.''

He swept her into his arms for a kiss that filled her, made her complete and let her know that she had finally met her match, found her soul mate, the man who would light her days and nights with love.

Epilogue

"I hear you just took a full-time job at Morning View Elementary School." Erica Taylor McCarthy sat across the picnic table from Elizabeth.

Elizabeth nodded and bit into a potato chip. "Starting in September, I'll be teaching third grade." She directed her attention to the distance, where Richard, Talbot and Andrew were playing catch.

It was hard to believe that almost a year had passed since Richard's surgery. Richard had just completed his first year of college and looked healthier and happier than Elizabeth had ever seen him.

"Has Richard decided what he wants to do yet?" She turned back to look at the woman Richard had married nine months before, a woman who was now seven months pregnant.

Erica smiled. "Not yet. Believe it or not, he's really enjoying his part-time work with the construction company. I wouldn't be surprised if eventually he starts up his own construction business." She smiled again and patted her bulging tummy. "Now that he knows this is a boy, he wants to build a big, elaborate tree house in the backyard."

Elizabeth laughed, then directed her attention back to the men. A smile curved her lips as she watched her son jump with hand overhead to catch a wild ball thrown by Talbot.

Initially, she'd worried about Andrew and how he would handle her relationship with Talbot. But Andrew had been surprisingly accepting of Talbot in his mother's life, and Erica in his father's.

He shared a true father-son relationship with Richard, but enjoyed a closeness with Talbot, as well. She'd heard Andrew boasting to his friends that he was really lucky. He had the best dad *and* the best stepdad.

Elizabeth's diamond ring caught a shaft of sunlight and sparkled brightly. While Richard and Erica had enjoyed a huge wedding with all the trimmings, a month later Elizabeth and Talbot had gotten married in a small, simple ceremony.

She had been Mrs. Talbot McCarthy for eight months—the happiest months of her life. And the happiness had only increased when three months after the wedding she found out she was pregnant.

Andrew was thrilled at the prospect of not one, but two siblings soon to arrive. He intended to be the best big brother in the whole wide world.

She smiled as the guys finished their game of catch and approached the picnic table where she and Erica sat. "Did you guys work up a healthy appetite?"

Talbot sat next to her, looking disheveled from his earlier exertions. "I think I worked up a healthy case of exhaustion." He caught his breath and grinned at her. "That kid has some arm on him."

"Yeah, but I need to practice batting," Andrew replied as he grabbed a handful of chips from the opened bag.

"We'll do a little batting practice after we cook the hamburgers," Richard said. He grabbed the platter of patties and smiled at his son. "You gonna help me cook these?"

"Okay," Andrew replied.

"I'll come with you," Erica said. A moment later the three of them walked the short distance to the grill.

Talbot took the opportunity to kiss his wife. "How are you doing? You feel all right?" He placed the palm of his hand against the swell of her stomach. "Hello in there. Everything okay?"

Elizabeth laughed and covered his hand with hers.

"We're both doing fine. And we've never been happier."

He smiled the sexy smile that fired a flame inside her. "You've never looked prettier. You positively glow. I've always heard women do that when they're pregnant."

Elizabeth smiled at him. "That's not a pregnancy glow. It's a love glow."

"I love you, too." He leaned forward and kissed her again, gently, softly. "You are the best thing that ever happened to me," he said when the kiss ended.

"I feel the same way."

For a moment they sat side by side, watching Richard, Erica and Andrew cooking the hamburgers and laughing together.

"He's a different man than he was a year ago," Talbot said softly.

Elizabeth smiled at her husband. "We're all different than we were a year ago." She knew she was. Being married to Talbot had opened a new world of sharing as she'd never shared before, and that sharing had created a wonderful, special bond with the man she loved.

"Will you be disappointed if this baby is a girl?" she asked.

He eyed her in surprise. "Why would I be disappointed? I'd love a little girl just like her mother, with butterscotch hair and bright blue eyes."

"And what happens if she has bright blue hair and butterscotch eyes?" Elizabeth teased.

"I don't care if she has purple hair and orange eyes. I'm going to love her as I do you—with all my heart."

Tears sprang to her eyes, tears of joy. She was so incredibly lucky. Her life was filled to the brim with happiness. Her hand reached for his and she smiled as his fingers curled around hers.

She had a sister-in-law who was sweet and kind, an ex-husband who was one of her best friends, a son who was well-adjusted and bright, and Talbot—the man who made her heart sing with passion and laughter and love.

* * * * *

*Don't miss Carla Cassidy's
newest release*

MAN ON A MISSION,

*available next month from
Silhouette Intimate Moments!*